'So, with all our suspects on duty tonight, let's hope for all our sakes we get a result.' The chief issued his command to Bella.

With an end possibly in sight, Bella could feel her newly acquired confidence diminishing rapidly. Her mind was whirring as she made her way to work, going over and over her own mental notes, checking and rechecking her theory just to be sure she was right. As much as she would have loved to dwell on the thought of seeing Heath at work later, tonight was just too big for any diversions, no matter how appealing. But she allowed herself one tiny luxurious glimpse, one grateful sigh that hopefully soon this would all be over, that soon she'd be able to tell Heath the whole truth, and hopefully he'd understand about her police work, understand why she'd had to go undercover. Then she could really start life over again...

POLICE SURGEONS

Love, life and medicine—
on the beat !

Working side by side—and sometimes hand
in hand—dedicated medical professionals
join forces with the police service for
the very best in emotional excitement!

From domestic disturbance to
emergency room drama, working to
prove innocence or guilt, and finding
passion and emotion along the way.

UNDERCOVER AT CITY HOSPITAL

BY
CAROL MARINELLI

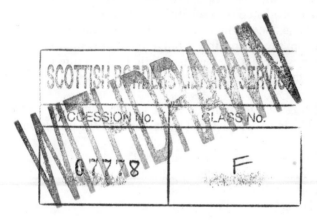

MILLS & BOON®

First published in Great Britain 2005
Large Print edition 2006
Harlequin Mills & Boon Limited,
Eton House, 18-24 Paradise Road,
Richmond, Surrey TW9 1SR

ISBN 0 263 18852 3

Set in Times Roman 17 on 19 pt.
17-0106-44443

Printed and bound in Great Britain
by Antony Rowe Ltd, Chippenham, Wiltshire

CHAPTER ONE

'YOU know that you don't have to accept this assignment, Constable Gray?' Inspector Eddie Bandford did his best impersonation of a friendly yet professional smile and Bella did the same, reminding herself to keep her hands neatly folded in her lap and to stare her senior in the eye. A natural fidget, it took Bella a supreme effort to do what seemingly came naturally to most people over the age of five—sit still for five minutes! 'You know,' Inspector Bandford continued, his voice so assured, his platitudes so emphatic Bella almost believed him, 'that if you decided this isn't for you, in no way will it impact on your application to be a detective.'

'Absolutely.' Bella nodded, her response equally emphatic, her clear green eyes unblinking as she stared assuredly back. 'But I

5

want to do this, Inspector Bandford. In fact, I'm thrilled that I'm even being considered.'

Another friendly yet professional smile.

Another pause as he eyed the file in front of him, and had she had a bell in her pocket, Bella would have been sorely tempted to ring it, to call for some time out.

Cut the bull, Eddie, she wanted to snarl. *You know as well as I do that if I turn this down, my application to be a detective will be fed into the shredder by the time I hit the lifts. You know as well as I do that the only reason,* the only reason, *I'm being considered for this role is that I happen to have been stupid enough to keep my nursing registration up to date and that I'm practically the only cop in Melbourne who can work my way around the inside of an emergency room instead of hovering in the waiting room.*

'It doesn't worry you?' Inspector Bandford closed the case file and picked up another, flicking through it with agonizing slowness as Bella felt her stomach turn to liquid as her senior read through her personal record. 'Going back to nursing, I mean. I understand you left because—'

'Because I realised that I wanted to be a policewoman,' Bella broke in, her voice amazingly even, nodding when he looked up to affirm her point. But even with a hefty dash of assertion added to her words still she registered the tiny flicker of doubt in Inspector Bandford's expression and moved quickly to quell it. 'That all happened years ago,' Bella said firmly, waving an almost dismissive hand at the personal file he was holding. 'I dealt with all that long ago.'

'But even so…'

She could hear the hesitancy in his voice, her inquisitive eyes taking in the deepening frown between his eyes, and Bella pulled on every last reserve she had to drag out a small laugh.

'I thought you wanted me to take the job, Inspector.'

'No,' Eddie corrected her. 'I've merely asked you to come in here to discuss the possibility, that's all. Detective Miller and I both agree that this business with drugs going missing at Melbourne City has been going on for long enough. Unfortunately, all the usual channels of investigation have been exhausted. All the staff have been extensively interviewed, we've had surveillance in place from the waiting room, even hidden cameras in the drug room...'

'Which have been repeatedly sabotaged...' It was Bella breaking in now, her curious mind switching in an instant to the puzzle that needed to be fixed, focusing on the task that could be hers if only Eddie Bandford gave the final nod of approval.

'Clearly, from our observations it's someone senior that's taking the drugs.' After a long moment of hesitation he handed her a list of subjects and Bella snapped them out of his hand like an eager puppy taking a treat. 'Someone with good access...'

'Most doctors and nurses would have access to the drug cupboards,' Bella pointed out, but Eddie shook his head.

'Only a few very senior staff knew that we were installing cameras in the drug room. Not only that, most of the drugs have been taken soon after the pharmacist has stocked up the cupboards and there's a decent haul to be had. Whoever's taking the drugs knows what they're doing, knows exactly how the system works and knows that we're watching them.'

'Why has Dr Ramirez been ruled out?' Bella asked, reading down the line of suspects. 'He was the most likely suspect for a while and from this I can see why. He's the consultant of the department, recently lost a child, been involved in a major accident, there are a lot of stressors…'

'There are,' Eddie agreed. 'And, as you say, he was one of the prime suspects, until he headed off for an extended break in Spain and the thefts continued.'

'Shame!' Bella gave a rueful laugh.

Eddie reciprocated with one of his own, but as her eyes worked the list again they both went quiet. He did nothing to fill the silence, watching as his junior mulled the situation over, processed all the information she had been given that afternoon, chewing on her bottom lip in quiet contemplation, a hand that had been clenched in her lap moving to her head and automatically freeing a blond strand of neatly tied-back hair and twirling it around her fingers. If Eddie Bandford had had any doubts about the validity of sending in one of his uniformed constables as an undercover nurse, they wavered then—Isabella Gray *was* the natural born detective that she insisted she was on rather too many occasions. Petite, dizzy and terribly blond she may be, but that was a gift in itself. Not for a second would you imagine the razor-sharp mind behind that rather scatty exterior, the shrewdness behind those trusting green eyes, and perhaps more relevantly the aloofness behind that dazzling smile. Isabella Gray had, by police standards, the enviable natural ability to make people open up to her while giving away absolutely nothing of herself, coupled with a brain, that came up in just a few moments with an extremely pertinent observation.

'It all seems so calculated. You'd expect an addict to have made a mistake by now.' A tiny shake of her head, her strand of hair forgotten as she nibbled on her thumbnail. 'I mean, I know they can be cunning and manipulative, but this has been going on for so long that you'd think by now there would have been some clear sign there was an addict in their midst, some air of desperation, some sort of slip-up.'

'You would,' Eddie agreed, and Bella didn't even look up, staring over and over at the list before her. All the main suspects were highly qualified, all incredibly well respected by their peers. How sad that amongst this impressive list lay a thief.

'And the quantities…' Bella said, more to herself than to the inspector. They were talking a lot of drugs.

A lot.

The nursing part of her brain might be rather rusty, but from the figures before her there was more than enough going missing to feed one person's habit.

'Do we think they might be selling them?'

We.

It had been deliberate.

Slip in *we*, force her toe in the door just a touch, and subliminally let him know she was part of this now. But Eddie had been around the block too many times to miss a trick.

'*Detective Miller* thinks that's a distinct possibility.' Bella's cheeks went pink as Eddie gently pulled her back. 'Which is why he's taking the unusual step of requesting a nurse go in undercover. Only the CEO and one of the nursing supervisors would know. There's a chance after all that the perpetrator isn't on our list of suspects. But more to the point, the people on the list in front of you are, for the most part, well liked, respected and extremely trusted—the last thing we want is even a hint that whoever is sent in is anything other than a nurse, because otherwise someone will end up revealing it in supposed confidence.'

'Whoever?' Bella questioned, tired of the games now. She wanted this—badly. OK, after what had happened to Danny, she'd sworn she'd never step foot inside an emergency room as a professional, sworn she'd never go back to nursing, but she wasn't going back, Bella consoled herself. She was going forward, taking on a job that, if she performed well, would surely move her that difficult inch over the line to being accepted to train as a detective.

She *had* to do this.

'I haven't made my mind up yet. Look, Bella, I know you say that what happened in your previous nursing career is all in the past, that you're over it, but I'm yet to be convinced. This could be dangerous. As you've rightly pointed out, Detective Miller is leaning towards the possibility that these drugs aren't being used to sustain one person's habit, that this could be part of a drug ring, and I don't need to tell you how ruthless those type of people can be. Naturally there will be back-up, we'll have an undercover officer in the waiting room at all times, but even so, the last thing we need is to send someone in there with emotional issues—'

'I don't have issues,' Bella broke in forcibly. 'I'm not going to break down on the job, for heaven's sake. Surely you know me well enough by now to know that much.'

'I don't know you, though, Bella.' Eddie remained unmoved. The only concession was that he dropped her title and called her by her name. 'No one in the station really knows you. Sure, you're friendly, personable and well liked by your colleagues but, as we've discussed before, on many occasions, you never really let anyone in.'

'And as I've said—on many occasions,' Bella added dryly, 'has it ever affected my work? Has the fact I'm not exactly the station's social butterfly ever once impacted on my professionalism?'

'No.' Eddie answered, tight-lipped.

'Have I, even once, brought my problems to the station?'

'No.'

'So let me do this.' Bella leaned forward a fraction in her chair. 'I'm more than up to it.'

'I'll speak with Detective Miller some more and let you know. Thank you for staying behind. I know your shift should have ended an hour ago.' Eddie nodded to the door and Bella knew it was all she was going to get from him for now, knew that even though he'd invited her in to discuss the possibility of going in as an undercover nurse, this particular interview was far from over, and that appearing too eager, too needy wasn't going to help matters. Taking her cue, she headed for the door, the professional smile back in place. 'No, thank *you* for considering me, Inspector. I'll look forward to hearing your decision.'

'One more thing, Constable Gray. Have you ever worked at Melbourne City?'

Bella shook her head. 'I did my training in a suburban hospital.'

'So no one at Melbourne City would know that you left nursing to join the police?'

'I can't say for sure,' Bella admitted honestly. 'There's a big turnover in hospitals, people pop up all over the place. But my departure was fairly low key at the time. I guess there might be a few people who will recognize me, but they wouldn't know that I'd joined the police.'

'I'll bear it in mind.'

The interview was definitely over now. Eddie picked up his pen and started to write, clearly assuming that the door would quietly close, but Bella stood there until he looked up, and from the frown that formed he was clearly slightly irritated to find she was still there.

'I said I'd let you know, Bella,' he sighed. 'There's nothing more to say until I've spoken with Detective Miller.'

'But there is.' Her voice was clear, the compulsive fidgeting that was so much Bella still now, and from her stance Eddie knew that what Bella was about to say was non-negotiable, that whatever was on her mind had already been decided. Putting down his pen, he offered her his undivided attention.

'You said that if I get the role I would be going in as an RN?'

'That's right.' Eddie nodded. 'We could have put you in as a student or a nurse's aide but Detective Miller felt you'd have better access to the critical patients and senior staff if you went in as a fully qualified RN with a certificate in emergency nursing. And given that you've got all the credentials, Bella, we may as well use them.'

'Agreed.' Bella nodded. 'So long as you explain to Detective Miller that *if* I get the role, I will not compromise patient care under any circumstance. If I'm going in as part of the team, people will be depending on me…'

'You're a police officer,' Eddie started, but Bella shook her head.

'I'm a nurse, too. I want this, Eddie, you know how much I want this role, but unless we set down some ground rules, unless you and Detective Miller understand where I'm coming from, you might as well put a thick red line through my name. I cannot and will not compromise a patient in my care.'

'I think you're being a bit melodramatic here, Bella. You're only going to be there for a couple of weeks.'

'Have you ever done a shift in Emergency?' Two spots of colour flamed on her cheeks, but apart from that Bella kept her temper firmly in check as Eddie shook his head. 'Then take it from me, I'm not being melodramatic.'

Stepping out into the late afternoon sun, Bella dragged in a deep calming breath, but it didn't work, her heart rate still skipping along way too fast, her brain still reeling from the unexpected carrot that had been dangled before her.

Boarding a tram, she took her usual seat at the back, only this time she didn't eye her fellow travellers, didn't play her usual game of people-watching, guessing who everyone was and where they were all going. Instead, she rested her head against the window and tried to quell the flurry of nerves that danced inside her; tried and failed to envisage herself back in an emergency room; tried and failed to envisage her detective application going through if she turned down the role on 'personal grounds'. And yet…it wasn't just nerves that were dancing as Bella stepped off the tram and walked the five-minute distance to her destination. It was excitement—pure, unadulterated excitement.

She'd be going undercover.

Undercover!

Using her own mind, her own people skills, working out clues—in fact, being everything that she wanted to be...

Except a nurse.

Stopping at the milk bar, Bella bought a magazine and chatted to Sandra, the owner, for a couple of minutes. After a very respectable pause, which the two women knew was just for effect, she decided to spoil herself with a bar of chocolate as if it were an occasional treat, not a daily essential.

'How's Danny?' Ringing up the till, Sandra asked her usual question.

'Good,' Bella replied, just as Australians always did. Half the family could be being held at gunpoint and the answer would be the same.

Good.

'How's Danny?' Bella asked Tania, the young nurse who was feeding him, putting down her chocolate and magazines on his locker and pulling up a chair before taking over the bowl of puréed mince and vegetables.

'Good.' Tania smiled brightly. 'He's just not very hungry.'

'Still?' Bella sighed. 'He hasn't eaten much all week.'

'The doctor's been in to see him, he couldn't find anything wrong. He said we were to try giving him some nutritional supplements, there's some in the fridge, I'll go and fetch you one. Can I get you a coffee or anything?'

'I'm fine, thanks.' Bella shook her head, stirring the unattractive meal around the plate.

'Maybe later—with your chocolate perhaps?'

'Maybe later,' Bella agreed.

Another pleasant but pointless conversation, another pretence at normal that, even after all these years, merely felt false.

'How was your day, Danny?'

He didn't even look at her, didn't smile, didn't shrug, and didn't say 'good'. He didn't say anything at all, just let out a moan when Bella tried to persuade him to eat the shepherd's pie.

'Come on, Danny,' Bella pleaded. 'You *have* to eat something. If you don't, they're going to put the nasogastric tube down again and you know how much you hate that.' Lecture over, Bella forced a smile, rued the fact that even after all this time, even though she came in just about every single day, the mere sight of him could still bring her to the verge of tears. That gorgeous, athletic body, atrophied now, his blond sun-bleached hair that she'd loved so much, crudely cut now, courtesy of the mobile hairdresser more used to elderly clients. But Bella tried not to let her hurt show, tried so hard, just as she always did, to carry on chatting as if the person sitting opposite her was as animated and as interested in life as her, carried on chatting as if it were her gorgeous, vibrant, sexy fiancé she was coming home to. 'You haven't asked how I am! Well, I'm *good*, actually. Really good, in fact. You'll never guess what Inspector Miller called me into his office for today...'

CHAPTER TWO

'WELCOME to chest pain city!'

Acutely uncomfortable in her very new uniform, supremely conscious that at least one of her police colleagues was hovering out in the waiting room, Bella did her best to blend into the throng of nurses standing at the nurses' station as the night sister smiled up at them, no doubt anxious to get the hand-over started and finished as quickly as possible. But even though she'd been away from nursing a long time, Bella knew this was one handover that was going to take a while. One look around the chaotic department, one look at the weary faces of the night staff and Bella knew it had been a very busy night. Several doctors were around, writing notes, making calls, working in Resus, the waiting room lined with people still waiting to be seen.

Trolleys lay abandoned and unmade in the corridor, some still with rumpled blankets on top, a sure sign the night had been hell.

'How was your holiday, Jayne?' the night sister asked, and Bella looked over as a middle-aged woman rolled her smiling blue eyes, giving a dry laugh as she accepted the hands-free phone from the ward clerk and chatted for a moment before turning it off and placing it in her pocket.

'Great, Hannah—only now it doesn't feel as if I've been away. That was South Ward,' she added. 'They want to know if we can keep the patient they're expecting down in the department till after seven-thirty. They can't take him now because they're busy with handover.'

'Oh, the poor guy,' Hannah groaned, shaking her head as a porter pushed a trolley out of a cubicle. 'He's been here since ten last night.'

'Which is why I told South Ward that they were too late and he's already on his way up.

They'll just have to tear someone away from their half-hour sit-down and mug of coffee. Go on, Jim,' she called to the porter. 'Take him up.'

Normal, Bella decided on the spot, peering at the name badge pinned to the woman's crisply ironed blouse and confirming that it was indeed Jayne Davies. Her short, practical light brown hair was still damp from the shower, a slick of lipstick the only make-up she wore, and clearly, from the way a couple of doctors had already waylaid her to ask a question, the way she'd dealt with a ward's rather annoying request, even before hand-over had started, Bella knew that this was a woman very much in control.

But Hannah!

Bella's eyes worked the woman, taking in the rather jumpy appearance and wild hair, remembering the briefing she'd had from Detective Miller. A night sister, Hannah was working overtime to support her ailing husband, and apparently it was common knowledge around the department she had massive financial problems. But the weary smile she gave as she caught Bella staring, the tiny wink she imparted in a show of support for a nurse on her first day, had Bella shuffling her mental cards somewhat, discarding Detective Miller's observations a tad and deciding to form her own opinions. Right here, right now Hannah was way down on her list.

'I've let Bethany, the grad nurse, go home early,' Hannah said to Jayne. 'She's got her driving test at lunchtime and obviously wanted to have a sleep first, so we're a bit short on the floor at the moment. I haven't even had time to check the drugs.'

'OK, Trish.' Turning to a nurse standing next to Bella, Jayne gave out her orders. 'If you wouldn't mind, you can go and check the drugs with one of the night staff. I'll fill you in on the handover later. Something tells me that if Hannah wants to get off before lunchtime then we'd better get started now!'

Chest pain city was certainly an apt description, Bella thought as they made their way around the department. For various reasons, some obvious and some completely obscure, certain symptoms seemed to present themselves *en masse*. Christmas and New Year were notorious for fights, the dangerous combination of alcohol and distant relatives in close proximity enough of a reason, hips and wrists were top of the list on a frosty morning, and on a wet night you could rest assured a higher proportion of road accidents would be present. And as to the obscure: any night nurse would testify that the slightly mad were barking on a full moon, but chest pains? Why did they all seem to arrive at once?

The handover *did* take for ever, the world didn't stop in Emergency as it did on the wards. Ambulances still arrived, unstable patients still demanded vigilant attention, and one by one the entourage of nurses was trimmed down as Jayne allocated them tasks.

Finally the rather depleted group, comprising Jayne, Bella, a couple of students and Hannah, were at the end of the resus list. 'Charles Adams, seventy-four years of age, previous history of hypertension and angina.' Hannah suppressed a yawn as Bella peered over at the patient lying exhausted on the gurney and attached to various monitors. A woman by his side, dressed in a massive trench coat, held his hand. Bella assumed it must be his wife, watching anxiously as a very tall blond doctor took some blood from the patient's other arm, chatting away to both of them as he did so. Bella's interest upped a considerable notch and it had nothing to do with the fact that the doctor was completely and utterly stunning. It was because from the description she'd been given, she realised this must surely be Heath Jameson, the consultant she was investigating.

She was investigating!

Every now and then Bella felt as if everyone must surely know, as if surely there was some massive sign above her head telling everyone the real reason she was here, but for a moment or two Bella realized it had seemed as if the clock had turned back, as if she really was just another nurse on a busy Monday morning listening to handover.

Heath Jameson.

Summoning details to mind, Bella stared apparently nonchalantly as Hannah gave the handover.

Recently divorced, massive custody issues with his ex-wife over the children and a hint of partying rather too hard since being reluctantly made single, though apparently in recent weeks that had all calmed down. With the promotion to Acting Consultant, it would appear that Heath had settled down and decided to concentrate firmly on his patients and career. Certainly, from the way he was chatting to Mrs Adams, he was doing a good job, taking some time to reassure the anxious woman instead of merely rushing off.

'Charles woke this morning at five a.m. with central chest pain, radiating down his left arm. His wife Celia decided it would be quicker to drive him in than wait for the ambulance!' Hannah's raised eyebrows told everyone the unfortunate lack of wisdom behind that decision. Patients with chest pain could collapse very quickly and with no warning—and this, it seemed, had happened to Charles *en route* to the emergency department. 'Now, I should warn you at this point, just so that you're prepared, that there's no telling Celia what to do. She's read every article on the internet about her husband's condition and as I speak is no doubt suggesting to Heath what blood tests he runs. I tried to tell her that next time her husband gets chest pain, assuming that her husband survives this event, she should call an ambulance because next time there might not be a police car travelling behind her. Thankfully, on this occasion the police officers realized she was in trouble and forced her to pull over so they could assist. He went into VF just as the paramedics arrived.'

'Lucky,' one of the student nurses commented, and Hannah nodded.

'Very lucky! The paramedics shocked him once and he reverted to sinus rhythm.' She gave a small grin. 'And gave him some IV lignocaine as ordered by Celia! They basically got an IV bung in and scooped and ran, then brought him in, where he's carried on misbehaving! He was just about to be given some morphine and promptly suffered another VF episode. Heath's in with him now...'

'Why aren't Cardiology in with him?' Jayne asked. 'The man's had two cardiac arrests after all. Surely they should be down here.'

'Because they've had as bad a night as we have,' Hannah sighed. 'They're stuck on ICU with another chest pain who's had a full, extended arrest and a teenager who took every last one of her grandfather's heart tablets.

Heath is looking after him till they can get here.

'Problem,' Hannah said as a rather anxious-looking Trish returned.

'There's an ampoule of morphine missing!'

If Bella had felt conspicuous before, she felt as if she were glowing now, scarcely able to believe that after only half an hour in the department drugs were already missing. But her internal excitement was somewhat dampened by Hannah's response.

'Damn!' she cursed, instantly putting her hand up. 'That was my fault! We wasted the morphine Mr Adams was supposed to have prior to his arrest. Bethany and I signed for it but the patient got restless again as soon as he came round and Heath decided to go ahead and give the morphine but we'd already thrown it out. Bethany and I got a fresh ampoule but we were so busy we didn't have time to sign for it at the time. She's off duty now; I can ask Heath—'

'Who checked the drug?' Jayne broke in.

'Bethany and I.'

'So why would you get Heath to sign for something he didn't check?' Jayne's voice was crisp, her stare direct. 'Hell, Hannah, you know the trouble the department's been in with drugs going missing, you know we have to do things by the letter. You'll have to ring Bethany at home and tell her to come in and sign for it.'

'But she's got her driving test,' Hannah protested.

'And I've got a department to run,' Jayne clipped back. 'Now, I'm sorry to do this, Hannah, I know you've got the kids to get to school, but before you go off duty I need you to fill out an incident report.'

'What?'' Hannah's voice was incredulous. 'It's a non-event, Jayne. You're completely overreacting. I really can't stay. I need to have a couple of hours' sleep before I bring Ken back here for his outpatients appointment at eleven...'

'Sorry to interrupt, but could I have a hand in here, ladies?' A rather snobbish, very deep, very laid-back drawl halted the bickering, and Bella's eyes widened as she turned around. The reading on the heart monitor that had been blipping along slowly but regularly had reverted to the wiggly line of VF and Heath was laying Charles Adams down before he even passed out, before his wife had even registered that there was something really wrong. As Trish dashed over and led her away, Heath was applying fresh pads to the patient's chest as Jayne quickly pressed a button to charge up the defibrillator. The machine whirring into action was a sound Bella hadn't heard for ages, but as instantly memorable as a dentist's drill.

Heath was supremely calm, an utter contrast to Bella who could feel her heart fluttering almost as much as the patient's—watching in awe as Heath pulled the paddles out of their trays.

'Everybody back.'

Another memorable noise, listening as 200 joules were delivered to the patient, watching as his body spasmed, then turning to the monitor.

'Still VF. Charge to 360 and could someone put out a code?'

On the wards a code would have been called immediately, but events like this were more commonplace in emergency and they had the equipment and expertise to deal with it. Once Charles's heart had failed to respond, however, it was time to call for the team.

Heath's hands were on his patient's chest now, commencing cardiac massage as he called for drugs that would hopefully work on the irritable heart before they shocked him again.

'Bag him, please, Bella.' Jayne's order was sharp and to the point.

Hell, she hadn't even been shown around the department, but Bella knew that with the RN badge dangling from the cord around her neck she was responsible now, not an undercover cop but an emergency nurse, and a life was on the line.

An ambu-bag was already connected to the oxygen, lying on the head of the trolley beside the patient thanks to his previous episode. Bella checked the man's airway to make sure it was clear before extending the neck and placing the mask firmly over his face, delivering oxygen as the machine charged and Heath pumped on.

'OK. Everyone back,' Heath ordered, then addressed his patient. 'Come on, Charles. I've just finally managed to arrange a bed up on CCU for you. Don't let's waste it.'

As soon as Jayne delivered the shock, Bella took her position again, holding the bag tightly over Charles's airway, ready to commence immediately. Suddenly she felt resistance, the uplifting sound of the monitor bleeping, the unmistakable feel of the quiet tension that had been present seeping out of the room as Charles started thrashing his head around. Bella replaced the ambu-bag with an oxygen mask, letting out the breath she had been holding before finally looking up.

'It's OK, Charles.' Heath's voice was still calm, and he lowered his head and spoke into his patient's ear. 'You're back with us now. You just had another small turn.'

Which was one way of describing it, Bella thought, blowing skywards the hair that had escaped as she let out another deep breath.

'Fun's over, guys!' Heath grinned as the crash team started skidding into the room. 'This is Charles Adams, the patient I've been babysitting for you. He's just had his third episode of VF in the last three hours and this time he had to be shocked twice before he reverted. Can we get him out of here now please and onto CCU?'

'Good job, everyone.' Heath nodded to the staff, then addressed Bella. 'I assume from the way you reacted, you've done emergency before.'

'Not for a long while,' Bella admitted.

'Well, you did great.' He held out a hand. 'I'm Heath Jameson, the very new acting consultant.'

'Bella Gray.' Bella smiled. 'And I'm the very new nurse.'

'Welcome aboard.' Very green eyes smiled momentarily at her, but his face grew more serious as he looked away, nodding to the group to step outside Resus and addressing Hannah and Jayne.

'If you have to argue, could you do it well away from Resus next time?'

'I'm sorry, Heath.' Jayne blushed darkly. 'But you know the problems we've been having with drugs.'

'So does half the department now,' Heath retorted sharply. 'Is Bethany on duty tonight?'

Hannah nodded.

'Well, she can sign for the drug then and do an incident report when she comes in. I don't want my nurses half-asleep on the job, which is what she will be tonight if we drag her back here now to fill in a blessed incident report just to appease the powers that be. That's when real mistakes start to happen.' He turned to Hannah. 'If you can come in fifteen minutes early tonight, you can fill yours out then.'

Hannah gave a grateful nod but Jayne was far from appeased.

'Heath, this is a nursing-related issue and given that I'm the most senior nurse in the department...'

'This is a staff-related issue,' Heath corrected. 'And I'm the consultant. Sorry,' he added before Jayne could. '*Acting* consultant.'

'So you're pulling rank now, Heath? According to the records there are drugs missing...'

'There's a single vial of morphine that hasn't been signed for,' Heath broke in, instantly diluting Jayne's accusation. 'And if anyone has a problem with the incident reports being filled in tonight instead of this morning, they can discuss it with me. I am not having a simple mistake turning into a drama, and if it means pulling rank then I'm up for it. I am not going to walk around panicking about things and feeling guilty when I'm not, and neither do I expect the rest of the staff to. Now, can I have a nurse to come in to speak to Charles's wife with me?'

And turning on his heel he stalked off, leaving everyone, especially Bella, standing blushing and open-mouthed.

Jayne because she'd been put down.

Hannah because she'd been backed up.

And for the rest of the nurses standing there, including Bella, it was entirely due to the fact that they were female.

CHAPTER THREE

CELIA was inconsolable.

Sobbing in a chair, a massive overcoat over a fluorescent nylon nightdress, pulling tissues out of a box, she stood up and let out a wail of terror as Heath and Bella walked in.

'Please, don't tell me…'

'He's not dead,' Heath said quickly, taking her elbows and lowering her back into the chair. Bella could only admire him. Instantly he'd quelled Celia's greatest fear without giving false hope. How many other doctors would have walked in and quickly said that Charles was OK, that the drama was over when, in fact, it had barely started.

'This is all my fault.'

'It's no one's fault.' Heath attempted to soothe her. 'Charles has had a heart attack, and unfortunately these types of events often occur afterwards. He suffered another cardiac arrhythmia,' Heath explained. 'His heart effectively stopped again. However, we got it started.'

'And he's OK?' Celia begged, but Heath held back.

'He's critically ill, Celia, but we're moving him up to the coronary care ward and we've given him some drugs which we hope will calm his heart down. The next forty-eight hours will be—'

'Critical,' Celia whispered through chattering teeth. 'I've read all about heart attacks on the internet.'

'Quite.' Heath flashed a brief smile, clearly not impressed with her cyber-knowledge. 'For now, though, I need you to tell me what happened.'

'It's all my fault,' Celia said again. 'I should have listened to him when he said he wasn't well enough—'

'Did Charles have chest pain last night?' Heath asked, but Celia shook her head.

'He was fine last night. I made him a special dinner. I told him to forget his diet for a night, we had a bottle of nice red wine and everything was fine until this morning. Oh, God, what have I done?'

'This isn't your fault,' Heath said firmly, then softened it with a smile. 'Some doctors actually *recommend* red wine for cardiac patients and I can assure you, Celia, nothing in last night's meal would have caused this...' Clearly he'd said the wrong thing as her sobbing grew louder. Bella pulled out another wad of tissues as Heath struggled to say the right thing, his eyes meeting hers over the woman's heaving shoulders in a silent plea for help.

'It's OK, Celia,' Bella said soothingly. 'I'm just going to have a word with the doctor and we'll be right back.' Gesturing to the door, she walked outside and waited till he joined her, a quizzical look on Heath's face, clearly surprised that Bella had pulled him out at such a sensitive time.

'She's very upset.'

'Very,' Bella agreed, nibbling on the skin around her thumbnail. 'Extremely upset, in fact.'

'Well, I guess that's to be expected.' Heath shrugged, his frown deepening as Bella's eyes met his. 'Why did you call me out?'

'Because I think you were making things worse in there.' She heard him suck in his breath, clearly irritated that this very new nurse was pulling him up. But as a tiny smile wobbled on her lips as she tucked back a strand of hair behind her ear over and over, Heath finally joined the party, a smile of his own starting, eyes crinkling around the edges as he waited for her to elaborate.

'What am I missing, Bella?'

'The sexy night attire under her coat for starters.' Bella grinned, blushing as he did, too. 'The romantic dinner for two, the fact she's feeling impossibly guilty…'

'They're allowed to have sex,' Heath said gruffly. 'Just because they're in their seventies—'

'He's a cardiac patient,' Bella broke in.

'So? Just because he's got a heart condition it doesn't exclude him from having a healthy sex life.'

'Of course not,' Bella agreed, 'but you've seen the medication he's on at home. It wouldn't be surprising if he was having some difficulties with…' Clearing her throat, Bella attempted to squash her embarrassment. 'Maintaining an erection.'

'I'm not with you, Bella.' He gave her a rather wide-eyed look and made to go back to the room, but Bella stilled him with a sentence. 'She's an internet junkie!' Heath was frowning now, two vertical lines appearing on the bridge of a very nice nose as Bella continued. 'I'd suggest that Celia's guilt has nothing to do with the eggs she put into his soufflé or the wine she served, but more to do with the little blue pill she served up instead of after-dinner mints.'

'No!'

'Yes.' Bella nodded, her smile widening as Heath blushed to his impossibly blond roots. 'If you ask me, there's a very good reason Celia's feeling guilty, and you insisting that it wasn't her fault isn't exactly helping matters.'

'Do you think she drugged him?'

'Oh, please.' Bella laughed. 'I'd say she just nagged him to death more likely!' As Heath opened his mouth, Bella got there first. 'Pun entirely intended. Look, it's just a hunch, but if I am right, maybe you need to alter your line of questioning a bit.'

'Line of questioning!' Heath gave her a slightly startled look. 'We're in Emergency, Bella, not down at the local police station!'

'Of course,' Bella responded quickly. 'I meant—'

'I know what you meant.' Heath gave a grateful nod. 'And you're right, if Celia's been ordering drugs from the internet, then my line of questioning was way off track. How the hell am I supposed to broach this with her?'

It was more a statement than a question, and Bella watched as he raked his hand through his superbly cut hair.

Danny was blond.

At a totally inappropriate moment the thought popped into her head.

There was absolutely no comparing the two.

Danny had been the surfy, sporty type, with shaggy blond hair that had always been in desperate need of a cut, living his life in bathers and board shorts, whereas Heath was the epitome of cool sophistication. No doubt his wardrobe was full with variations on the superbly cut suit he was wearing now, just an occasional glimpse of subtle but expensive jewellery but wearing enough aftershave to asphyxiate from fifty metres.

There was no comparison, Bella concluded, *except for the fact they were both blond.*

'Hell, they never prepare you for this type of thing in medical school,' Heath moaned, staring directly at her.

And except for the fact they both had beautiful eyes.

'Or nursing school,' Bella agreed, heading back towards the interview room, frantically trying to clear these ridiculous thoughts from her head.

'How did you work it out?' Heath asked, catching her arm lightly and pulling her back. 'I mean, how did you guess what was going on?'

'Just incurably nosy, I guess.' Bella shrugged but she lost her audience as a red-eyed Hannah brushed past, clearly in tears.

'Hey!' Heath called her back. 'Jayne didn't make you stay and write that report?'

'No!' Though visibly upset, Hannah forced a smile. 'Just another stupid mistake I made last night—I left my car lights on.'

Heath gave a groan of sympathy.

'I've called the roadside assistance number but it would appear I'm not the only one. There's a two-hour wait.'

'Get a taxi,' Heath suggested, 'and then pick your car up when you come in for Ken's outpatient appointment. Shirley on Reception can tell roadside assistance where your car's parked.'

Raking her hand through her hair, Hannah gave a nervous nod. 'I guess. It's just…' Her voice trailed off, but Heath picked up the silence with efficient calmness.

'You're probably entitled to a cab charge. Why don't you check with Jayne?'

'I was just about to.' Hannah gave a pale smile and started to go, and only then did Bella really understand. A cab charge might get her home but she'd have to pay for a taxi back, and if funds were short perhaps the twenty or fifty dollars it would take hadn't been factored into this week's budget, let alone a new car battery and callout fee. But it wasn't Bella's place to say anything. She was the very new girl here, so instead she stood in polite silence, pretending not to watch this exchange.

'Hannah?' Heath called her back. Maybe he had understood, Bella realized as he dug in his jacket pocket and pulled out a very flash-looking keyring. 'Take my car.'

'Sorry?' Hannah looked completely dumbfounded as her weary face turned around.

'You're over twenty-five, I assume?'

'Way over.'

'Then take it.' Heath shrugged. 'Jayne's pretty tied up, you'll have to wait for ever for her to go into the office and find the forms. Just take my car.'

'Heath—'

'I'm not going anywhere,' Heath groaned. 'Just don't smoke in it.'

'I've run out.' Hannah grinned, the first real smile Bella had seen from her breaking over her exhausted face.

'Then there's no problem.'

And except for the fact that under all the bravado, both Danny and Heath were as soft as butter.

As Hannah happily made her way off, jangling Heath's car keys in her hand, Heath rolled his eyes heavenwards. 'Why me?' he groaned.

'I'm sure she'll look after it,' Bella ventured, referring to his car, but that, it would seem, was the least of his problems.

'I couldn't give a damn about the car. Why, out of all the doctors in the building, do I get the geriatric nymphomaniac to deal with?'

And except for the fact that they both made her laugh!

'Is everything OK, Doctor?' Celia jumped up as they entered, terrified eyes dragging between the two. 'Nothing has happened to my Charlie, has it?'

'No.' Heath gestured to the chair and waited patiently as Celia sat down, clearing his throat and staring at the floor for an endearing moment before assuming a bland expression and looking down at the woman. 'Now, Celia, for Charles's sake, I really need to know what happened last night. I need to know about any medications he might have taken, anything unusual that's happened recently…'

'There's nothing!' Celia said quickly, too quickly Bella thought, and clearly so did Heath.

'Celia, this is an emergency room. No one's here to judge either you or Charles. We just want to give your husband the best treatment possible and to do that we need all the facts. So if there's anything you can think of that might help, anything you're holding back, now might be a good time to tell me about it.'

'What about…?' Celia gave a nervous swallow. 'I mean, if I'd done something wrong…'

'I'm a doctor, Celia. My only concern is to see Charles gets the appropriate treatment.'

'And I won't get into trouble?'

Heath shook his head. 'I just need the truth, Celia.'

CHAPTER FOUR

'CAN I grab you for a moment, Bella?' Jayne clicked off the hands-free telephone as Bella came out of the interview room. 'I need to check some pethidine.'

'Sure,' Bella replied easily, walking towards the drug room with Jayne.

'How's Mrs Adams?'

'Better. Heath's still in with her. She's still upset, though. Oh, that's what I came out for. Where do I get tissues? There aren't any spare boxes in the interview room.'

'I'll get Tony onto it for you,' Jayne answered, swiping her ID on the drug-room door and waiting for the access light to turn green.

'The domestic?' Bella checked. 'Don't worry, I'll ask him. I actually want him to service the room while he's in there, it looks as if a bomb's hit it.'

'I'll speak to him about it,' Jayne said, fiddling with the drug cupboard keys then giving a rather weary sigh as she opened it. 'Remember to smile for the camera!'

'So it is true, then?' Bella asked innocently. 'Drugs really are going missing?'

'I'm afraid so. I'm sorry you had to find out that way but, with the way gossip spreads in this place, it's just as well that you know and can understand why everyone seems to be acting a bit strange at times. No one likes being under suspicion and until they catch whoever is responsible we're going to just have to live with it. It's awful, isn't it?' Jayne added. 'That's why I came on a bit strong out there. We have to be more careful, *have to*,' she reiterated. 'It's all very well for Heath to say I'm overreacting, but he isn't the one signing his name at the beginning and end of the shift in the drug records.'

'And there are really cameras in there?' Bella peered inside, staring at the neat rows of drugs and pretending to try and locate a lens.

'Not *in* there.' Jayne laughed. 'At least, not that I've heard. Up there.' She gestured to a small black box on the ceiling. 'It's supposed to be hidden, but everyone knows it's there.'

'Gosh.' Bella stared upwards, resisting a childish urge to wave to her colleagues.

'Anyway, it's nothing for you to worry about. Just make sure you check things carefully and don't be rushed. It's just common sense really.' Pulling out a box of pethidine, she opened the drug book. 'Pethidine, 100 milligrams. There should be nineteen ampoules.' Swinging the ampoules around in the package so the drug name was visible on each, she waited patiently while Bella checked. 'I'm taking one, which leaves eighteen.' They both signed off the drug book and safely locked everything away then Jayne collected a kidney dish and syringe as Bella watched. 'This is for a Mr Benjamin Evans, a forty-eight-year-old who was trying to put the roof on a pergola this morning and forgot to secure the ladder. He's hurt his back.'

'Ouch.' Bella grimaced.

'He's had X-rays and Jordan, the registrar, has had a look. The damage is muscular, so we're going to give him this and send him home in a couple of hours for a few days of bed rest.'

'One hundred milligrams?' Bella checked, looking at Jordan's writing, surprisingly neat for a doctor.

'He's a big guy,' Jayne responded, pulling up the drug into a syringe and placing it in the kidney dish. 'And a bit of a baby,' she added. 'You'll soon see.'

Walking towards the cubicles, Bella didn't need to be told twice who the medication was for—the groans coming from cubicle four spoke for themselves. But at that moment Jayne's pager shrilled loudly.

'Damn,' she cursed, glancing down at the little bleeper clipped to her blouse. 'I need to get this. Bella, go and tell him I'll be there in two seconds.'

'Sure.'

He certainly was a big guy. Mr Evans practically filled the trolley, but Jayne's rather mean description that he was a baby seemed a touch harsh, Bella thought as she introduced herself to the patient. He was in a lot of pain yet still he managed an understanding nod when Bella explained there was a bit of a hold-up with the medication.

'It shouldn't be too much longer, Mr Evans.'

'Ben.' He grimaced. 'It's my own stupid fault anyway. That'll teach me to go climbing ladders.'

'Just think.' Bella smiled, happy to make small talk to keep his mind off the pain. 'In a few weeks this will all be behind you and you'll be sitting under your lovely new pergola, having a nice cold beer.'

'If I ever get the roof on the damn thing!'

'Sorry about that, Mr Evans.' Jayne bustled in, waving the kidney dish and prescription chart as Bella checked the patient's name band.

'Benjamin Evans, ID number 1514103.'

They both checked the name band and drug sheet, making sure the identity matched before turning to the drug order.

'Pethidine 100 milligrams,' Jayne confirmed, and Bella nodded. 'OK, Mr Evans, just a small scratch.' Swabbing his thigh, Jayne slipped in the needle and delivered the powerful drug, before carefully disposing of the needle and syringe in the sharps box on the wall. 'Now, that should take a little while to start working, but once it does, you'll be feeling a lot more comfortable.'

''Thanks, Sister.'

'You were *very* nice to her,' Bella said a couple of hours later as Heath wandered into the staffroom, where she stood attempting to read the instructions on a massive vending machine and rueing the fact that the five-dollar note in her hand wasn't going to fit into the coins-only slot.

She meant it.

After the initial discomfort Heath had guided the trembling woman through the event, listened as she'd told them how she'd bought the tablets from a 'doctor' on the internet, sure this would be the answer to Charles's little problem.

And he'd been wonderful, gently explaining to Celia that the tablets she and Charles had purchased could, in fact, be dangerous in the wrong hands, that Charles's cardiac condition meant he wasn't suitable for that type of medication. However, he'd gently said, it didn't mean it wasn't treatable, that with a sympathetic *real* doctor they could, when Charles was better, resume a fulfilling sex life.

'And very well informed on erectile dysfunction too,' Bella added with a cheeky smile, giving up on the vending machine and heading for the massive tin of brown powder that supposedly passed as coffee and pulling out a mug to wash from the overflowing sink.

'I was about to buy you a coffee,' Heath responded, not remotely fazed by the below-the-belt humour nurses lived by—police officers, too, come to that. 'But if you're going to be like that, I guess I'll just have to watch you suffer.' He fed a dollar coin into the machine and Bella listened as it whirred into motion, the delicious smell of coffee beans reaching her nostrils as Heath stood watching his cup fill, jangling his loose change in his suit pocket. 'Are you going to take that back?'

'Absolutely.' Bella smiled, weakening instantly, the smell of coffee just too good to resist. 'I think there's algae growing in that sink. Doesn't anyone ever wash up here?'

'No,' Heath said, and Bella could have sworn there was an edge to his voice. 'But whenever I say anything, apparently I'm nagging.'

'Says who?'

'Jayne!' Heath rolled his eyes. 'Apparently, since my temporary promotion I've become picky, that if I were just a bit easier on the domestic staff they might stick around a bit longer. The place is falling apart and I'm not supposed to notice!'

'Do you have change for a note?'

He rolled his eyes and fed a dollar into the machine then headed off, leaving Bella to make her selection. If she had just been a nurse the conversation would have ended there—the polite small talk made around the coffee-machine, a fifteen-minute break from outside activity definitely what was needed now—but, with her police ID burning a hole in her pocket, Bella consoled herself as she dragged him away from his newspaper that she had to do this, had to force a conversation, had to get to know him a bit better.

She wasn't flirting!

Just doing her duty.

'Thanks.' Holding up her plastic cup, she sat on a couch on the other side of the room.

'No problem.' He flashed a perfect smile and promptly turned back to his newspaper.

'My shout next time. Once I get change, of course.'

'Fine,' Heath responded without looking up.

'It's been a busy morning!' Bella said brightly, wincing inside as Heath visibly sighed and put down his paper, clearly giving up on any chance of a quiet cup of coffee.

'How are you finding things on your first day?' Heath asked.

'Great,' Bella said eagerly. 'Everyone's been really friendly, except, of course...' Her voice trailed off and she waited for Heath to jump in to seemingly instigate a conversation she needed to have.

'This morning's little altercation?' Heath gave a tight shrug. 'I'm sorry you had to hear that on your first day. Normally the department's very friendly and easygoing, but things have been a bit tense lately.'

'Why?' When Heath didn't immediately respond, Bella pushed harder. 'Are there really drugs going missing from the department?'

'Unfortunately, yes.'

'A lot?'

Heath gave a grim nod. 'Enough for the police to be involved.'

'Really!' Bella's eyes widened suitably.

'All the staff were interviewed a few weeks ago and it seemed to settle down for a while, but it seems to have started again. That's the reason Jayne was so worried this morning when the morphine was unaccounted for.'

'You weren't,' Bella pointed out, watching his reaction as Heath gave an easy shrug.

'Because there was a logical explanation. Last night was hell down here. I was called in at three a.m. because the department was stretched to its limits. It's no wonder Bethany and Hannah didn't get a chance to sign for the drug, and I certainly wasn't about to see poor Hannah stuck here filling in an incident report after the night she's had and Bethany hauled out of bed for a simple, honest mistake.

'Anyway, it's nothing for you to worry about. Just understand that people are a bit on edge at the moment and, for goodness' sake, make sure you check and sign for everything.'

'Well, thanks for explaining.' Bella smiled, but any chance of prolonging the conversation had to be aborted when the senior consultant, Martin Elmes, walked in and Heath, who had been lounging on the couch, sat up just a touch straighter as his boss came over.

'Sorry to do this at short notice, Heath, but would you mind giving the doctor's talk this morning? I've got a slight touch of laryngitis.'

'I'd be glad to.' Heath beamed.

'Nothing too in-depth. I know I haven't given you much notice. Just something light and interesting, perhaps generate a discussion. I'd like to hear some of the new interns open up a bit, find out if we've actually taught them anything!'

'No problem at all,' Heath responded as Martin made his way out, the smile rapidly disappearing as the door closed. 'I'll give him bloody laryngitis,' Heath mumbled.

'His voice did sound a bit husky.'

'Because he smokes a pack a day,' Heath countered. 'How the hell am I supposed to come up with something "light and interesting" on two hours' sleep?'

'You could have said no,' Bella pointed out.

'I don't think so somehow.' Heath gave a wry grin. 'Not if I want to drop the *acting* part from my job title.'

Bella gave a sympathetic groan as Heath stood up, recalling her own false enthusiasm when Eddie Bandford had first suggested this role. She watched as he drained his coffee in one gulp then stretched, not even attempting to cover a massive yawn before heading for the door.

'I wonder how many more Celias there are out there?' Bella called to his departing back.

'Sorry?' Clearly distracted, Heath flashed her an irritated look over his shoulder as he reached the staffroom door, no doubt wondering if this blessed nurse ever stopped to draw breath.

'I was just sitting here wondering how many more patients there are ordering drugs from the internet or delaying coming to Emergency because they're self-diagnosing on the net.'

'Hundreds probably,' Heath muttered, that hand raking through his hair again, those dark green eyes creasing endearingly as his mind ticked over. 'Thousands even.' A smile crept over his lips. 'And if it does nothing else, erectile dysfunction always raises a smile.'

'Light *and* interesting.' Bella grinned back, picking up a magazine from the couch and settling in for the five minutes before she was due back on duty. And normally she'd have devoured it, normally she'd have flicked straight to the back and scanned the pages for her horoscope before turning to the fashion section, but instead she just held it, staring blankly at an ad for deodorant, feeling a vague fluttering in her stomach that hadn't been there for almost as long as she could remember.

She liked him.

Really liked him.

Liked the way he'd stood up to Jayne, liked the way he'd spoken to Celia, liked the way he'd put down his paper and spoken to her when all he'd clearly wanted to do had been to read…

She really liked him.

A trembling hand came up to her lips and Bella screwed her eyes closed for an uncomfortable moment, wishing she could somehow erase that thought, guilt stinging the edges. She didn't want to like him, didn't want to complicate her world that way. She was here to work not just one but two jobs, here to concentrate, to make sure the thief was caught. Heath might even be the thief.

But all that she could deal with, all that she knew she could take in her professional stride…

Her guilt was solely reserved for Danny.

'Still no better?' Bella asked sympathetically, checking Mr Evans's blood pressure. She frowned in concern when he shook his head, his face screwed up in pain.

'Maybe a little bit. That second injection you gave took the edge off a little, I guess.'

'That was Voltaren—it's an anti-inflammatory,' Bella explained.

The pethidine hadn't helped at all, and after discussion with Jordan, the registrar who was looking after him, it had been decided to give the patient an anti-inflammatory. But Mr

Evans was still in a lot of pain and clearly not in a fit state to go home. 'The orthopaedic doctors are going to come and have a look at you, but in the meantime our consultant has decided to give you some more pethidine.'

'It didn't help at all.'

'I know, but you are quite a solid build...'

'That's a polite way of putting it.'

'Look, we'll get a urine sample from you just to check there's no renal damage.'

'I already did one.'

'Well, it can't hurt to check again,' Bella said in a matter-of-fact voice, producing a bottle from the side of the trolley for Mr Evans. 'I'll just wait outside.'

'What's going on?' Heath asked as he strolled past, doing a double-take at the groans coming from behind the curtain.

'He's just doing a urine specimen, then I'm going to get him that pethidine.'

'Jordan's already said the urine's clear,' Heath answered briskly, clearly already versed in the case. 'Come on, Bella, the guy's in agony. Can we, please, just get him the pethidine that Jordan ordered and hopefully get on top of his pain some time today?''

'Can you check it with me, then?' Bella asked, ignoring his rather sarcastic comment. 'Everyone else is tied up at the moment.'

Heath's drug checking wasn't anywhere near as thorough as Jayne's, tapping his foot impatiently as Bella counted the drugs, signing his name in an impatient flurry then practically galloping across the department to get the job done.

'Let's hope this helps,' Bella said sympathetically as they rushed through the ID checks, Heath darting outside before the needle was even in the patient in a race to get back to wherever he might be needed.

'There's that specimen you asked for.' Ben gestured to the bottle on the locker by the trolley. 'I couldn't do much, I'm afraid. Will there be enough?'

'I'm sure there'll be plenty.'

CHAPTER FIVE

'SHOULDN'T you be at home?'

Rummaging through her bag for a stethoscope, bracing herself for her second day on duty, Bella caught sight of Hannah puffing on a cigarette in the tiny courtyard outside the staffroom. Pushing open the door, Bella popped her head around.

'I should be, but I just wanted to have a word with Heath when he arrived about Mrs O'Keefe. I promised the poor woman at midnight we'd soon have her vomiting under control, and the poor thing's only just stopped retching.'

Bella gave a sympathetic smile, perching herself on the white plastic seat opposite and deciding that, given the department was quiet, no one would miss her for five minutes or so and to spend that time trying to get to know Hannah a little bit better. 'She's the woman with the breast cancer and secondaries in her lung.'

'Poor darling.' Hannah nodded. 'She's just finished her final round of chemotherapy and has come over from Ireland with her children to spend some time with her sister. Dr Jenkins, the oncologist, has told her that she ought to think about going back to Ireland early.'

'He's discharged her back home to her sister's, hasn't he?' Bella checked. 'Her husband's just taken the tram home to fetch the sister's car.'

'He has.' Hannah grimaced. 'But I'm still hoping we can do something more for her. She's only forty-five, the same age as Ken. My husband,' Hannah added, by way of explanation. 'He's got MS.'

'I'm sorry.'

'Not half as sorry as I am. He's a miserable old git at times.' Hannah gave a wry smile. 'But I love him to bits.'

'Is that why you do nights?' Bella ventured. 'So that you can spend the days looking after him?'

'Heavens, no!' Stubbing out her cigarette, Hannah rolled her eyes. 'I do nights purely for the extra money. Ken's pretty right during the day, he's got the district nurse coming in, and a couple of days a week he goes to a support group at the community center. I hate leaving him in the evening. It's the one time of the day we can actually forget for a little while that he's got MS. The nights I'm off we sit in bed watching a movie, drinking hot chocolate...' She gave a fond smile. 'Mr O'Keefe just struck a chord with me. Apparently her specialist wasn't very hopeful about his wife's chances. She hasn't had a followup CT scan yet but I think deep down he knows that she might only have a few weeks left and he just wants them to be as normal as possible for her and to really enjoy this holiday. He wants her to be able to have an ice cream with her daughter, take her along the pier in her wheelchair. It shouldn't be too much to ask.'

'It shouldn't,' Bella agreed. 'But at least they've stopped the vomiting.'

Hannah shook her head. 'For now. They've given her some Kytril.' She watched as Bella frowned at the unfamiliar name. 'It's an anti-emetic and,' she added, 'a wonder drug at times, it can eliminate nausea and vomiting in some cancer patients, you wouldn't know it unless you worked on the oncology wards. It costs a lot of money and Dr Jenkins has given her a script for it, but there's no way they can afford to get it dispensed and their insurance doesn't even begin to cover it. Apparently they had a lot of trouble getting travel insurance to come away and anything related to her cancer treatment isn't covered. I asked Dr Jenkins if we could get a course dispensed from the hospital pharmacy, at least enough to get her home, but he said no.' Hannah gave a tired sigh. 'I can understand where he's coming from, of course, there have to be guidelines and we can't just give expensive drugs out like lollies, but it just seems such a shame, that's all. I guess it all comes down to money in the end.'

'So what can Heath do?' Bella asked.

'Bend the rules.' Hannah shrugged. 'He's a good egg usually. I know a few people would say otherwise...' She smiled at Bella's obvious curiosity. 'He went a bit off the rails when his wife left him. Stood on more than a few toes around the department.'

'In what way?'

'He forgot that there isn't the letter ''I'' in the word ''team''. He'd been turned down for the consultant's position and took every available opportunity to prove what a mistake they'd made.'

'Heath?' Bella checked, surprise evident in her voice.

'You know how fragile men's egos are.' Hannah winked. 'His wife had left him and

I guess Heath thought his career was in the toilet...'

'I hear that you're after my wallet!' Bella jumped as Heath came to join them outside. His blond hair was damp, undoubtedly from his shower, and a heavy waft of the after-shave he didn't believe in rationing preceded him. 'Is it for Jim's leaving present?'

'I'd forgotten about that.' Hannah fished in her bag and pulled out a rather tatty brown envelope. 'I'm actually struggling a bit with this. I think people gave a lot for Dr Ramirez's present when he went on extended leave. Jim's our night porter,' Hannah added for Bella's benefit. 'He's part of the furniture actually. He's been here for forty years, since the very first day the department opened!'

'Here.' Peeling a very generous note from his wallet, Heath dropped it in. Hannah duly noted it on the front as Heath went to go, but Hannah halted him.

'It wasn't actually Jim's present that I wanted you for, Heath.'

'Why don't I like the sound of that?' Pulling up a chair, he sat down. Glancing at her watch, Bella knew that she really ought to be heading outside, but this was exactly the type of conversation she needed to listen to and, deciding to risk Jayne's wrath, chose instead to stay. 'Is there a problem with Ken?'

'For once, no.' Hannah smiled at Bella, still taking care to include her in the conversation. 'I've called on poor Heath for a few favours in my time. Actually, it's about Lucy O'Keefe, the terminal patient in cubicle four.'

'I've just spoken to Dr Jenkins about her. She's going back to her sister's, isn't she?'

'With a script for Kytril that she can't afford.' Hannah stared almost defiantly at Heath. 'There's a drug that works for the poor woman and we can't give it. It's the same with Ken...'

'Let's not get onto a cannabis debate,' Heath groaned, and from the way he said it Bella had the feeling it wasn't the first time they'd discussed it. Legalizing cannabis for treatment in terminal patients and certain diseases was a topic that reared its head every now and then but, despite common consensus that it did have some merit, currently in Australia it was still illegal. 'They are doing trials in New South Wales, Hannah, but at the moment it's still an illegal drug and you and I alone aren't going to change that fact!'

'Even though it works for MS patients,' Hannah responded hotly. 'Even though it's the one thing that actually gives my poor Ken...' Her voice trailed off, but Bella's ears were agog! That innocent cup of cocoa in bed with Ken at night was taking on a whole new slant now!

'Let's keep to the point,' Heath said gently, but Hannah had the bit between her teeth now.

'The point is, Heath, there is a *legal* proven drug that can help this woman, give her a chance to finish her holiday, have a few more dignified days with her family before she heads back to the UK to die, and because of budgets and bureaucracy all we can give her is a single dose. Lucy could bend the rules. She could come back every blessed day vomiting her head off and you know as well as I do that we'd have to give it to her.'

'No doubt you've told her that.'

'I have,' Hannah admitted. 'But unlike some of the timewasters we see in this department, hospital is the last place poor Mrs O'Keefe wants to be. If you write the script on the back of the casualty card, we can get it dispensed...'

'And the emergency budget will have to cover it,' Heath pointed out. 'There have to be limits, Hannah.'

'Do you think I don't know that, Heath? I work within the rules four nights a week, but you know as well as I do that every now and then...'

'We break them.' Heath finished for her, but Hannah refused to buy it.

'I'm not asking you to break the rules, Heath, just bend them a bit.'

Letting out a sigh Heath read through Doctor Jenkins notes carefully before pulling out his pen and writing the scrip on the back of the casualty card. As straightforward as it might have looked, Bella knew it wasn't an easy choice. Every last cent had to be accounted for and Heath would be questioned for this later, but at the end of the day the three people sitting at the table knew he was doing the right thing. 'I'll give her ten days' supply, but no more, Hannah. Pharmacy isn't open till nine so I'll have to ring the on-call pharmacist and explain, and no doubt he'll want a registered nurse to go and collect them.'

'I'll go,' Bella offered.

'Well, dodge Jayne,' Heath warned. 'She's like a bear with a sore head lately. You'd think it was coming out of her own purse sometimes.'

'And watch your back.' Hannah laughed, clearly elated that Heath had listened to her plea and gone that extra mile. 'I might just mug you on the way back. They'd more than pay for my car battery.'

Wandering through to pharmacy, Bella was met by the grid-iron roller doors and pushed the intercom button, giving her name and department, before the iron rollers were lifted and a pharmacist who actually looked like a pharmacist unlocked the door, peering over his half-rimmed glasses at her, grey hair sticking up all over the place.

'This is for the doctor's mother, I assume?'

'Excuse me?' Sure she'd misheard, Bella frowned in confusion.

'Or is he just a really nice guy?'

Realizing he was referring to the rather generous prescription, Bella gave a nod. 'The latter, at least I think that's the case, but this is only my second day.'

'Well, don't just stand there—come through.' He waved cheerfully and Bella smiled at his slight eccentricity, waiting patiently as he locked the doors behind them. 'Ignore the mess. I'm afraid we can't get the staff these days.'

He wasn't joking. Bins were overflowing and the floor was sticky as Bella walked along.

'As it's only me here, you'll have to check them with me,' the mad pharmacist called out to her, jangling keys and pulling open cupboards as Bella peered around, realizing in an instant why no drugs went missing from Pharmacy. Everything was behind metal grids, not a single pill or ampoule in sight, and the pharmacist carefully locked the cupboards behind him before bringing the precious cargo over.

'Sit down,' he said. 'I'll need you to sign for them. 'OK, Kytril tabs...' he said, as Bella sat down. Peeling open the box, he showed her the contents and Bella nodded her agreement, signing on the page he offered. 'I need your initials here as well.'

Peeling off a label, they both initialled it, before it was stuck on the box.

'Signed and sealed,' the pharmacist boomed, handing over the box.

'Well, then, I'd better deliver it.'

And delivering it was a sheer pleasure. Reminding Bella for a sentimental moment of the really special times nursing could bring. Lucy O'Keefe's gaunt face broke into a tearful smile as Bella slipped the drugs into her handbag.

A tiny woman, despite her illness she was still very attractive with high cheekbones and sharp blue eyes topped off with a gorgeous lilting Dublin accent. Thanking Bella profusely as she rearranged her pillows and held the cup while she had a sip of tea, Bella knew there and then why Hannah had developed a soft spot for this patient. Even the cruel ravages of cancer couldn't take away her inner beauty, and not for the first time Bella realized how randomly cruel life could be at times.

Here was a mother, a wife, a daughter and a sister, and she didn't deserve to be leaving them all so soon.

'There's ten days' supply there, Lucy. That's all we can give you I'm afraid.'

'That's more than generous.' Pushing away a plate with a tiny bony hand, she leant back on the pillow, the brightly colored scarf tied around her head not quite enough to put colour in her cheeks. 'Have you any idea how good that slice of toast tasted?'

'You're the first patient I've heard praise hospital food.' Bella smiled.

'It's the simple pleasures you miss the most,' Lucy sighed. Instinctively almost, Bella took Lucy's hand, the nursing instinct that had been buried so long coming back as familiar and welcome as a lifelong friend you hadn't seen in a while. 'That medicine is not just for me,' Lucy sighed. 'Patrick and Marnie, she's my daughter, get such a kick out of me eating. They're always mashing bananas and trying to tempt me and it's not that I don't want to, it's just that I can't keep anything down.'

''These will help,' Bella said, knowing that medicine might work wonders, but so did positive thinking.

'They will.' Lucy smiled. 'More than you know. Can you thank the doctor for me? What was his name?'

'Heath.'

Both women looked up as a deep voice answered her question.

'Aren't you the man?' Lucy smiled. 'If I had any eyelashes left, I'd be winking at you, Doctor.'

'I was told you were a happily married woman,' Heath gently scolded.

'Nothing wrong with a bit of harmless flirting. But thank you, Doctor.' Her voice wavered. 'I really mean that.'

'No. Thank you,' Heath answered. 'Sometimes we all need a good kick up the backside to remember what we're really here for, and you, Lucy O'Keefe, have effectively delivered.'

'I'm good at kicking backsides,' Lucy said. 'Or I used to be.'

'Enjoy the rest of your holiday,' Heath said softly, taking the hand Bella wasn't holding and squeezing it for a moment. 'And if you need us, we're here.'

'Aren't you a love?' Lucy smiled. 'And I bet you've got a gorgeous wife and kids waiting at home for you.'

'I wouldn't call my ex-wife gorgeous.' Heath winked, happy to indulge in a bit of private chit-chat with such a delightful patient, knowing it would make her feel so much more than a number. 'But the kids certainly are.'

'Divorced!' Lucy's mouth gaped open. 'What was the woman thinking?'

It was a very good question and one that buzzed annoyingly in Bella's mind for the rest of the day.

At every turn he was gorgeous.

OK, a touch pompous, Bella decided, watching him talking to the medical students, clearly relishing in his acting consultant role, but there was an elusive quality to him that Bella only managed to define at the end of a long shift, pulling out her ponytail and stifling a yawn as she leant over his shoulder and signed on the casualty card he was writing for a tetanus shot she had given, that generous splash of aftershave still vaguely present.

'Finished?' Looking up, he smiled. It was a totally innocent remark, but Bella felt her insides literally flip over, could feel his breath on her cheek, caught the vague scent of a mint he was chewing on, saw the fan of lines around his eyes that surely hadn't been there that morning.

What *had* Heath's ex-wife been thinking?

'Who on earth did your off-duty?' Jayne stared at the roster with an appalled expression on her face, sipping at a coffee and trying to catch up on paperwork before the shift ended.

It was Bella's third exhausting day on duty.

Exhausting because she'd spent two hours at the station the previous evening, going over her findings with Detective Miller.

Exhausting because she'd arrived at Danny's nursing home still dressed in her nursing uniform and had had to lie to his tense, anxious parents as to why she was working in Emergency again, simultaneously reassuring them that the doctor who had examined their son that day surely knew best, that if he couldn't find anything wrong with Danny, maybe they didn't need to worry.

Exhausting because she'd sat up till midnight, watching hours of security video footage that Detective Miller had laughingly called her homework as he'd handed them over.

Exhausting because when finally she'd fallen into bed, instead of sleeping, she stared at the ceiling, her mind constantly drifting to the one thing she shouldn't even be considering.

Heath.

If she'd been a real nurse, she could have avoided him, and she would have, Bella knew that, would have gone to great pains to be terribly busy whenever he needed a hand, to ask Jordan to write up anything she might need. But instead, because she was undercover, because she needed to gather all the facts, her second day in the department had been spent following him around like a lost puppy, bending his ear for the most stupid of questions and generally making a complete idiot of herself when all she'd really wanted to do was hide. The very last thing she wanted to do was get to know Heath any better, spend even a single moment alone with him, because, quite simply, her feelings terrified her.

Since Danny's accident no one had even sparked a vague interest, yet within two minutes of meeting Heath she'd felt this sudden awareness, as if every hormone that had laid dormant for ages had somehow awoken.

And not slowly either.

No stretching and yawning and a few strong coffees to get them moving.

Just sitting bolt upright, fizzing through her veins and doing the strangest things, like making her blush, making her drop things, making her acutely aware of the fact she was very much a woman.

'No wonder we can't get any staff if this is how Admin's going to treat them. Have you seen the off-duty?' Calling Bella over, Jayne tutted loudly as she stared at the roster. 'You've got four early shifts this week then they've got you down as working on Saturday night. I don't even want to tell you what they've given you next week—you might pack your bag and walk out!'

'It's fine, Jayne.' Peering over her shoulder, Bella stared at the roster. 'Admin have already run it by me. In fact, I volunteered for the Saturday night—I need the money at the moment.'

The prepared and practised lie rolled easily off Bella's tongue. The last thing she wanted was for Jayne to change her shifts around. Every last one had been carefully worked out, taking both the medical and nursing roster into consideration. Even the intern who was supposed to be working on Saturday night had been given the night off to ensure that Heath stayed firmly on the hospital floor and in full view of Bella!

When she'd left Eddie's office after the first initial interview, Bella had expected to be kept on tenterhooks for a few days at least, but she'd barely got home from seeing Danny when her telephone had rung and Detective Miller had introduced himself to her; carefully explaining why things had been brought forward. Several of the main suspects would be working together over the next couple of weeks and that it might be prudent for her to start on Monday. At any given time she was working with the maximum number of suspects, and next week she was down to work nights alongside Hannah, with Jayne putting in an appearance for a couple of them and Heath the consultant on call. But from the way Jayne's eraser was poised over the roster, all the careful planning was about to be rubbed out. Even though Admin would change it back, it could only look suspicious.

'It's just too many shifts, Bella.' Jayne looked up. 'There's no point burning yourself out. A Saturday night in Emergency is hard at the best of times.'

'You're doing it,' Bella pointed out.

'But I'm off then till Wednesday.' Jayne frowned, her eraser poised over the paper.

'I'll be fine,' Bella assured her. 'Look, Jayne, I really need the cash.'

'And I really need nurses who are awake.' A deep voice that most definitely wasn't

Jayne's made Bella jump, and she blushed as she realized Heath had just heard her practically beg, but she was saved from any further discomfort when the red alert phone buzzed on the desk and Jayne promptly answered it, nodding at Heath to stay put for a moment as she took the details.

'Bike versus truck,' she said grimly to the gathering staff alerted by the emergency phone's buzzing. 'Major head injury and leg injuries, intubated at the scene. GCS 3. I'll put out an emergency page for the orthos. Trish, could you take Bella and start setting up?'

She didn't need this, Bella thought with a sinking heart as she headed swiftly to the resuscitation room.

Really didn't need this on only her third day back!

GCS stood for Glasgow coma scale, a rudimentary screening tool that assessed the seriousness of a head injury. The highest score was 15 and perhaps surprisingly the lowest score wasn't zero but three.

One point for eyes closed despite painful stimuli.

One point for zero motor response to pain.

One point for no verbal response.

And the patient that was coming in had the lowest score possible.

The same score that Danny had had.

Forcibly she pushed that thought away, demanded her brain concentrate as she prepared the trolley along with Trish, checking the oxygen and suction, pulling up drugs, running through drips and finally stepping back slightly as the paramedics dashed in with the unfortunate victim, a first glimpse of the black leather trousers, shredded around the thighs, his hands a mangled, bloody mess.

'On my count,' Heath called, taking the head end of the patient and assuming the role of leader, especially important with major injuries. The leader oversaw the entire process, co-ordinating the different teams while ensuring the stability of the patient's neck. The lift over from the stretcher to the trolley was swift but controlled, the anesthetist taking over the patient's airway. Trish and Bella took one side each, with specially designed scissors ripping through the leather gear the motorcyclist wore, shearing off his protection gear to allow the doctors better access.

'We took the helmet off at the scene.' The paramedic was sweating profusely, the heavy jacket and exertion of an extensive resuscitation not exactly light work in the mid-thirties heat outside. 'His airway was blocked and he needed to bc intubated. According to his licence and the check police did, his name's Andrew Stevens, thirty years old. The police are going round to his house now.'

Heath nodded, flashing a pupil torch into the man's eyes.

'Left pupil's fixed and dilated, right pupil's pinpoint.' His gloved hands felt the man's skull, and from the expression on Heath's face it wasn't good news. 'Boggy depressed fracture at the posterior.' He shone the torch into the man's ears. 'Blood in both ear canals. How are we doing at your end, Simon?'

'Compound fractured femur on the right,' the orthopaedic registrar said grimly, accepting a massive wad of sterile, saline-soaked drapes from Bella and placing them over the exposed fracture. 'Same again with the tibia on the left.'

'His heart rate's down,' Bella observed as she covered the fracture with the drapes, checking the pulse in his groin with her gloved hand. 'Very poor output.'

Heath looked over to the screen, checking the patient's pulse himself before nodding to Bella.

'Commence cardiac massage.'

The patient was a large, strapping man, probably twice Bella's size, and for cardiac massage to be delivered effectively, it needed all her weight behind her. Climbing up on the gurney, she knelt beside him, feeling for his sternum then lacing her fingers together and placing the heel of her hands in the right position before starting the massage, leaning over the patient and pushing down rhythmically, counting in her head and listening as the cardiac monitor bleeped regularly now.

'Good output with the massage,' Simon confirmed as Heath ordered more drugs to be pushed through the IV line in effort to pick up the heart rate. The whole resuscitation was being delivered effectively, yet there was a tension in the air that hadn't been there that morning. Charles's cardiac arrest had been the 'good' kind to have, a fibrillation, that could generally, if picked up early enough and treated promptly, be countered, but all the signs for this young man were atrocious and everyone knew it.

Bella was actually glad to be giving the massage, glad to be playing a role she knew she could do well, glad that her hands were knotted together and no one could see them shaking, and because cardiac massage was as exhausting as an aerobic workout, glad of the excuse to be red in the face and slightly breathless.

Why?

Staring at the lifeless body beneath her, she asked questions over and over.

Why did horrible things like this have to happen? Why was a young, fit man lying wasted and practically dead? As the resuscitation stretched on ominously, another question was raising itself. Why were they continuing with this?

Heath was clearly thinking along the same lines.

'OK, Bella, take a break.' It was the third time he'd done it—taking over the massage to allow her to catch her breath and give her aching arms a rest—but it wasn't a matter of Bella simply stopping and getting off the trolley. Heath moved his hands near hers and Bella waited till he gave the nod that he was ready to take over, his height and strength meaning he didn't need to climb up on the trolley, but it was important for patient care that the handover was done as smoothly as possible…

Even if there was little hope.

'It's three-forty guys.' He looked at the massive clock on the wall, which had been started as soon as the massage had commenced. 'We've been going for forty minutes with no response. We have to ask ourselves at this point if we do get him back what…?' He paused as the receptionist walked in, obviously embarrassed when everyone looked over at her, but Heath called her over, carrying on the massage as he addressed her.

'Have we got any more details, Shirley?'

'His wife and parents just arrived. I've put them in the interview room. There's a policewoman with them.'

'Thanks, Shirley.' Heath stared down at the young man for the longest time before continuing. 'Can someone take over? I'm going to go and talk to the wife.'

Bella nodded, putting her knee up to climb back on the trolley, but Heath shook his head.

'Someone else should do it, Bella, you've been going for ages. You can come and speak to the wife and parents with me.'

Appalled she froze, literally froze for a second, not even moving as Jayne came over to climb up onto the gurney, the thought of going into the interview room, of listening as Heath broke the shattering news, watching the family's reaction, reliving the absolute worst time of her life, almost more than she could bear.

'I'm off in twenty minutes.' Her voice was barely a croak. She felt as if her throat were full of shards of glass as she plucked at the stifling air for any available excuse. 'Perhaps it would be better if one of the late staff went in with you and I carry on with the massage. I really need to finish at four.'

It just didn't happen.

Emergency nurses didn't just walk away, no matter what the time, and everyone present knew it. Apart from the sounds of the monitors the room suddenly fell silent as

Bella stood with her cheeks flaming, painfully aware of how shallow she must sound as Heath stared angrily back, a muscle galloping in his cheek at her apparent callousness.

'I wasn't *asking* if you'd like to join me, Sister, I was *telling* you to come. A fresh pair of arms are needed to deliver effective massage and, given that the place is fit to burst out there, I don't have the luxury of staring at the roster for ten minutes to work out who's on late shift and who's in a rush to get off duty.'

Nodding to Jayne, his hands lifted as she took over the massage. He checked the patient's output for a moment before heading out of the resuscitation area and turning angrily to face her when Bella joined him.

'Have you got another job to go to?' he snarled.

'What?'

'You're cramming in as many shifts as you can because you need the cash. I heard you, remember. So do you have another shift to get to?'

'Of course not,' Bella said.

'So what the hell was all that about?'

'I'm sorry,' Bella started. Tears were dangerously close but she blinked them back, aware that her colleagues in the waiting room were undoubtedly watching the exchange, but also determined not to break down. 'I just thought it might be better for the family if they got used to one nurse...'

'He's going to die, Bella. Unfortunately, for Andrew and his family, it isn't going to take very long at all, but of course, if they get too emotional, if things drag on a bit in there...' He flashed a nasty, completely false smile as he started to walk. 'I'll try to hurry things along for you.'

'Heath...' she started, but even before he turned around she shook her head. Even if it might be better to explain things to him, there simply wasn't time. 'Your shirt's got blood on it.' She gestured to a massive linen trolley.

'Maybe you should change it before we go in.'

'Thanks,' he said almost grudgingly, staring down at the stained arms of his white shirt as Bella selected a theatre top. She half expected him to nip into a toilet or the staff-room, but, given that time was of the essence, Bella wasn't particularly surprised when, completely unselfconsciously, he ducked beside the trolley out of view of the waiting room and proceeded to pull off his shirt, taking the blue theatre top Bella handed him and tossing his shirt into a plastic bag. He handed it to a passing porter who took it without comment or wisecrack, the whole department slightly subdued, knowing what was taking place.

Walking in silence, they reached the interview room and Heath paused for a second, his hand ready to knock. He cleared his throat then dragged in a deep breath before turning to face her, the animosity gone from his eyes now, just two colleagues needing a bit of moral support from each other.

'I hate this part.'

Bella gave a grim nod. 'I know.'

And she did.

Knew how he felt as he sat down and introduced himself but, worse, far worse, she knew exactly how the family felt, their eyes raking the medical staff, desperate to glean some information before the verdict came.

'Andrew was brought into the department nearly an hour ago,' Heath started gently, 'suffering multiple injuries. He was deeply unconscious on arrival and his heart stopped beating effectively soon afterwards.'

'He's dead, isn't he?' Kathryn Stevens's voice was hollow.

'Kathryn.' Heath was careful not to shake his head, careful not to offer false hope. 'For over forty minutes now we've been trying to resuscitate Andrew, to get his heart started, but unfortunately we've had no response. None at all,' he added, very gently but very firmly. 'It is my opinion that if we were to get Andrew's heart beating, and at this stage I doubt very much we will, but if we were to, it would only be a matter of time before it stopped again.' He paused for a moment, letting the horrible news sink in as Andrew's parents clung to each other, the wife Kathryn so alone on a chair.

'If it didn't?' she whispered. 'I mean, if he survived?'

Heath nodded as she voiced her question. 'If Andrew were to survive this event and I have to say again that I don't think it's at all likely, then I believe he'd be severely brain damaged. He has massive head injuries, he was deprived of oxygen at the scene of the accident and there has been no response whatsoever to our vigorous resuscitation.'

'So what now?' She stared almost defiantly at him. 'What am I supposed to do now?'

'Would you like to see him?' Bella said gently, and Heath gave a small nod to show he thought it was a good idea.

'Please,' Kathryn agreed, but Andrew's parents shook their heads, sobbing helplessly as Bella stood up.

'I'll let the staff know that you're coming and I'll be back for you.'

There wasn't much that could be done in the short space of time to make Andrew look better, a blanket placed over his body to cover some of the injuries and mess, but it wasn't about making the moment more palatable, it was about giving Kathryn the opportunity to somehow process how seriously injured her husband was, to show that despite the fiercest of efforts there really had been no response.

'He's gone, isn't he?' Bella held on to the shaking woman as she stroked her husband's head, most of the staff standing respectfully back, except for the anaesthetist who ventilated him and Jayne who was still giving the massage, tears in her eyes, because even if emergency hardened you, even if you saw it nearly every working day, no one could fail to be moved at the tragic end to a life. 'He's got an organ donation card.' Kathryn looked up urgently at Heath. 'He was really adamant about it, said that if he were ever in an accident he wanted to donate his heart.'

'If we stop the massage,' Heath explained gently, 'then Andrew's heart will stop.'

He didn't go into details too complicated right now for Kathryn to comprehend, just gently let her know that Andrew wasn't going to make it upstairs to the intensive care unit.

'But he really wanted...' Kathryn started, and Bella felt her crumple beneath her hands, saw Heath's expression as Jayne stopped the massage under his command and the line on the monitor went flat.

'Kathryn,' Bella said firmly, holding the woman's shoulders, 'if that's what Andrew wanted, then there are still ways to respect his wishes. Some organs can be retrieved after death...' If her words sounded brutal they were needed, painful honesty no worse than the truth now. 'But we can talk about that later. Right now I think you need to be with Andrew, you need to say goodbye.'

CHAPTER SIX

'SORRY.'

Heath caught up with her as Bella came out of the staff changing room, pale, slightly red-eyed and emotionally exhausted.

'I'm so wrapped up in the place, I sometimes forget people actually have a life outside. When you said you were off at four, I thought—'

'It doesn't matter.' Bella shrugged, anxious to get away, to step out into the evening air and drag in a couple of deep cleansing breaths, to get into her car and put as much space as possible between herself and the hospital.

'But it does,' Heath persisted. 'It's past six. I should have realized that once you went in the interview room, you wouldn't just be able to walk away, that you'd have to see it through.'

He was trying to say the right thing and only making it worse.

She'd never been a clock-watcher. The fact it had been near the end of her shift had been nothing more than a hastily thought-up excuse so she wouldn't have to go and face Andrew's relatives. But more worrying to Bella was the fact she actually wanted to tell Heath how she was feeling. For the first time in years she actually wanted to tell someone just how bad she was really feeling, to open up a touch and let them take the weight for a moment, for someone to understand...

But she couldn't.

'Heath.' She forced a smile, made herself look him in the eye. 'It's no big deal.'

'You didn't have somewhere you needed to be?'

Bella gave a wry smile. She could hardly tell him she'd had to make a hasty phone call in the changing rooms to tell Detective Miller to send the back-up in the waiting room home and that she'd give him a report tomorrow. When he'd asked if she had any ideas, was any closer to working out who it might be, Bella had deliberately been vague, not quite ready to reveal what she couldn't quite articulate even to herself.

That she'd already made up her mind.

Already knew who was taking the drugs.

'Thanks for staying.' His hand brushed her elbow, a tiny squeeze that was probably just to show he meant it, but Bella felt as if she'd been branded with a hot iron, could feel the heat radiating through her jacket, almost claustrophobic as he stared down at her.

'Tony.' As the domestic walked past, glad of the diversion, Bella called out to him. 'Could you, *please*, make sure the interview room's sorted out properly? I've had relatives in there this evening, and the bin still hadn't been emptied or the tissues replaced.'

'I'm off now.' Tony gave a nonchalant shrug.

'Well, can you pass it on to the evening staff, then?' She sucked in her breath in irritation when he didn't answer, just ambled away. 'Tony!' she called out, but Heath put his hand back on her arm, pulling her back before she went too far.

'Leave it, Bella. Deal with it tomorrow.'

'Oh, I'm sure I'll have to,' Bella snapped. 'The place is a dump. I've never had to speak to an ancillary staff member like that. Normally they're falling over themselves to be helpful, especially down in Emergency.'

'He's just a kid, twenty at most.'

'I was two years into my nursing degree at twenty,' Bella retorted sharply, then bit her tongue, the whole wretched day catching up with her now. 'Look, I'm just tired, it's been a long day. You're right. Now's not the time to be getting cross over a box of tissues.'

'You're OK?' Heath checked.

'I'm fine,' Bella said, hitching her bag a touch higher, trying to wrap up the conversation, to move away, but her legs wouldn't obey her. In fact, her mouth was working overtime, prolonging a conversation when she should really just get the hell out of there. 'I'm actually glad in a strange way that I stayed. I know it was the right thing to do.'

'You were really good with her, I mean *really* good with her. You seemed to know exactly what to say or, more to the point, what not to say.'

And if Bella was having her own internal conflict, suddenly Heath was, too.

Staring down at her, her newly brushed blond hair falling in a fluffy cloud around her shoulders, a pale linen jacket over her uniform, massive green eyes on the verge of tears, he wanted to scoop her into his arms. Was hit for the first time in ages with a need that had become unfamiliar.

Not the lust that had forced his attention every now and then since his wife had left, a hunger that was easily satisfied but always left him with a bad taste, but a need to delve deeper, to take this suddenly fragile woman and get to know her, to delve a bit deeper.

'Bella, are you OK?'

She shook her head, put her hand up between them as he reached out to comfort her, stood there proud and lonely for a painful second before finally she looked at him.

'Sorry. It's just…'

'Just what?' Heath pushed, but again she shook her head, clearly not ready to reveal whatever it was that was on her mind. 'Do you want to talk about it?'

'Yes,' Bella admitted, 'but I can't.'

She was making to go, clearly embarrassed at having revealed so little of so much and all he knew was that he didn't want her to leave, all he knew was that he had to lighten the moment, had to put a trace of a smile on that taut mouth.

'You owe me a coffee, remember?' He delivered his line with an easy smile, almost resigned to the fact that she'd toss it straight back, that this chameleon-like, complicated woman would wave his offer away, but he felt his breath catch in his throat when slowly she turned, that deliciously full mouth breaking into the beginning of a smile, couldn't quite believe it when she teasingly shook her head.

'I'd say it's you who owes me, Heath. And a bit more than a coffee. I hear your ''internet'' lecture went down very well!'

What on earth was she doing?

Watching as Heath ordered drinks at the bar, Bella was tempted to grab her bag and run. How, she tried to fathom, as he made his way over, had that happened? One minute she'd been on the verge of tears, desperate to get in her car and escape, and the next she'd been flirting, *flirting* with Dr drop-dead, newly divorced, gorgeous Jameson. And not just flirting, but cocking her head in a poor impersonation of Princess Di and demanding not just a coffee but a real drink at a real bar.

A real date, even?

'Cheers!' Holding his beer Heath chinked her glass of wine and Bella took a grateful sip, consoling herself that they were in the hospital social club, that surely this was merely overtime, almost convincing herself even that she'd instigated the whole thing solely to investigate things further.

Please!

As his eyes met hers, as a tentative smile escaped from behind her glass, Bella knew the only person she was kidding was herself.

'I'm a bit rusty.' Heath put down his glass and gave an apologetic grin. 'I haven't done this in a while.'

He must have registered Bella's slightly raised eyebrow as she put down her own glass.

'I actually haven't, contrary to the hospital grapevine, spent the last year working my way through the nursing roster.'

'The last year?' Bella checked as if she didn't already know, trying to blot out what she knew from Detective Miller, trying to block out the whispers she'd heard in the three days she'd been at Melbourne City and judge for herself the man sitting in front of her. 'So what happened last year?'

'You don't miss a trick, do you?' He gave her a slightly quizzical look, but it was tempered with a smile. 'Sometimes I feel as if you've got a little notepad in your pocket, it's like I'm being interviewed or something.'

Bella did her best attempt at a dismissive laugh, cheeks flaming at her near miss. 'You're not the only rusty one,' she shot back, desperate to douse any suspicions he might have. 'I'm sorry if my bar-side chatter isn't particularly flowing.'

'I was joking,' Heath responded. 'Although getting to know someone these days does seem rather more complicated.' He registered her tiny frown. 'Do you know why most teenagers and twenty-somethings are so good at idle chatter?'

'No.'

'Because they haven't got a load of baggage to get through first. It's a lot easier to make small talk when there aren't any skeletons rattling in your closet. By the time you hit my age—thirty-four,' he added as Bella opened her mouth and snapped it closed again, determined not to render this a full on investigation, 'there's generally a few rattling around in there. Bad relationships, messy divorces...'

'Gay,' Bella sighed, as Heath laughed. 'The fish in the sea don't seem quite so plentiful once you hit thirty.'

'Well, I'm not gay, that's one skeleton not rattling in my closet, waiting to get out. I'm actually divorced.'

'I'm sorry,' Bella responded, because something in his voice told her it had really hurt.

'So am I.' Long fingers were running around the rim of his glass. 'And before you ask, no, there was no one else involved.'

'So what happened?' She gave a tiny wince, aware that she was asking too many questions. 'I'm just interested.'

She was, and it had nothing to do with a drug investigation!

Heath gave a small shrug, but it wasn't dismissive. 'We both wanted the same thing, both adored our children, both liked the nice things in life, and given I was the one working I was the one who had to put in the hours.'

'Too many?' Bella suggested gently.

'Way too many,' Heath admitted. 'I had it in my head that once I reached consultant, once I'd finally made it, I'd pick up the ball and run with it, catch up on all that I'd missed out on, but—and this is with two years of hindsight—I realize now I forgot to ask Jackie if she was OK with that. Sav, he was a registrar like me, put in both our applications when a consultant position came up, but instead of going home to celebrate I found out that Jackie was leaving, and not only that—she was taking the kids as well. I fell apart, and Sav got the job.'

'Dr Ramirez?' Bella checked.

'I hated him for a while,' Heath admitted. 'Pure jealousy. There was Sav, three beautiful kids, a wife who adored him and the consultant's position I'd dreamed of for years…'

'It's always hard,' Bella said, 'seeing people happy when your world is falling apart.'

'Trouble is, it was Sav that fell apart.' Picking up his drink, he took a long sip. 'His youngest son died. The guy was like a zombie, and who can blame him? And what did I do? Instead of supporting him, I used every opportunity to undermine him, to show how wrong *they* had been not to have chosen me. Pathetic as it sounds, I was jealous that everyone felt sorry for him. The poor guy had lost his child—'

'So had you.' Bella broke in, 'You'd lost your family, Heath, and maybe you deserved a bit of sympathy, too.'

He stared into his glass for the longest time, finally dragging his eyes up to meet hers. 'I never thought of it like that.'

'He's in Spain now isn't he? One of the girls told me,' Bella added.

'His wife had another baby, a little girl. We sorted out our differences. Sav's a great guy and now I'm trying to get back on track. I went a bit off the rails for a while, too much partying. Figured if they didn't think I was responsible enough to be a consultant then I'd damn well enjoy myself.'

'And did you?'

'Oh, there was the odd highlight.' He gave a small smile but it failed to meet his eyes. 'But, no, all in all, it's been a pretty crappy time.'

'And what form did this partying take?' Bella asked, suddenly nervous. She could almost feel his honesty, was sure that what came next would be the truth, and she didn't want her theory as to who was responsible for the drug thefts to be suddenly blown out of the water, but for more reasons than just her career.

She didn't want it to be Heath.

'The usual.' Heath shrugged.

'Drinking, women...' she picked up her glass, tried to sound casual. 'Drugs...'

'Mum! I didn't expect to see you tonight!' Heath grinned, then relented slightly. 'Yes to the first two, though, believe me, it wasn't as excessive as you're imagining, and a re-sounding no to the third. I'm not *that* down on myself. How about you?'

'Ah, I haven't hit the magical thirties yet.' Bella smiled. 'I'm still in the idle chit-chat stage.'

'Could have fooled me,' Heath said softly. 'Something tells me there's a lot going on there.'

'Nothing,' Bella answered brightly. 'I'm a crushing bore, actually.' Draining her glass, she went to pick up his, used to picking up her round with her fellow officers. 'Do you want another one?'

'Not here.' Heath rolled his eyes in the general direction of the bar. 'We're already the live cabaret. This innocent drink will be all over the hospital by the morning.'

'"Dr Jameson's up to his old tricks again."'

'Do you want to go somewhere else?' His voice was light, but Bella could felt the beat of hesitation. 'We could have dinner, though you'd have to drive, I'm afraid. I haven't got my car.'

'You've lost your licence?' Bella asked, shocked that she wasn't already aware of that and disappointed all at once.

'You've really got me pegged as a no-hoper, haven't you?' Heath groaned. 'No, I actually got driven in at seven a.m. courtesy of flashing blue lights. There was a car crash this morning on the freeway. The hospital rang and the police came and got me.'

'Oh!'

'So how about dinner?'

Regretfully, Bella shook her head. 'How about I give you a lift home?'

She could feel it—feel the tension crackling in the air around them as she drove her very old Fiat through the darkening streets. Everywhere coupledom beckoned, patrons spilling out of cafés onto the pavements, music pounding from bars as they stopped at every single red light, and it would have been the easiest thing in the world to flick on the indicator, to pull over and get out, to share a meal with a man who seemed to be growing more divine by the minute.

But it was as impossible as it was complicated.

Heath knew absolutely nothing about her, was still a suspect in a crime she was investigating. Absolutely no good at all could come out of it.

'Booze bus.' His voice broke into her thoughts and she let out a low groan as the all-too-familiar sight of police flagging down motorists came into view, a couple of empty cars by the side of a large white bus proof that even after all the adverts, all the warnings, people still hadn't quite got the message.

'You're being pulled in.' Heath grinned but it changed to a frown when he saw her anxious eyes. 'You had one glass of wine at the social club,' Heath pointed out.

'I know,' Bella mumbled. 'I just always feel guilty somehow.'

'Well, you've got nothing to worry about. Unless...' Heath grinned '...you've got a bottle of vodka stashed in your bag.'

Cheeks flaming, she waited her turn, cursing herself over and over for agreeing to go out with Heath without back-up. If she was being followed, the detectives behind would be radioing urgently ahead, warning the officers to just let her through, not to make a personal comment that would show they recognized her. She could see Andy, an officer she'd worked alongside on many times on

nights like this, waving a driver on and sig-
nalling her to come forward, and with her
pulse pounding in her temples Bella wound
down her window, registering the smile on
Andy's face as he recognized his colleague's
car.

'Hello, you!' he started, but as pleading
eyes met his, his cheery greeting petered out.

'Evening, Officer,' Bella said through impossibly dry lips, praying Andy would get it,
would realize that she was in fact undercover.

'Been working?' Andy asked, his eyes
flicking over the uniform.

'That's right.'

'And have you had anything to drink this
evening?'

'One glass of wine,' Bella croaked, pretending to listen as he relayed instructions,
licking her lips and trying to catch enough
breath to breathe into the blessed machine.

'Fine.' Andy nodded, checking the reading
and stepping back from the car. 'Enjoy the
rest of your evening.'

'He was friendly,' Heath commented as they drove off, and if ever Bella had needed a wake-up call then she'd got one, any thoughts of prolonging the evening flying out of the still open window as she followed Heath's directions, gratefully pulling up at a smart townhouse, thankful that this dangerous liaison was nearly over.

'Do you want to come in for a coffee?' His voice was gruff, and Bella could have sworn that even in the darkness she could see his cheeks darkening.

'Better not.' She kept her voice deliberately light, tapping her fingers on the steering-wheel as he unclipped his belt, feeling the weight of his stare burning into her cheeks as he turned to face her.

'Bella?'

She didn't want to turn around, didn't want to look at him, terrified, truly terrified he'd read the desire blazing in her eyes, make it more impossible than it already was to end the evening with a casual goodbye.

'Bella?'

This time she did turn, this time she did look at him, and she could see the slight trepidation in his own eyes at what was happening, the speed at which their feelings had taken over, and it actually made her feel better, the fact that he was as bewildered as her.

Heath's face was moving towards her with agonizing slowness, plenty of time to dodge away, but instead she was leaning forward, filled suddenly with a strong need to feel the weight of his lips on hers. She closed her eyes as that moment came, relishing the delicious scent of him, the warmth of his lips moving slowly on hers. She was vaguely aware somewhere in the periphery of her mind of her hand reaching out behind him, fingers burying themselves in the thick, silky blond hair, dragging him a touch closer, a delicious shiver somewhere deep inside as his tongue softly parted her lips, taking the intimacy deeper, tasting him, losing herself completely in the moment, the scratchy feel of his beautiful face against hers, the giddy, almost weightless feel his kiss aroused. She wanted to stay like that for ever, wanted his touch to drown out the pain of the past. But like an unwelcome visitor, reality beckoned, summoning her back to earth with a thud. Pulling away was the hardest part, ending the most precious, delicious moment she had indulged in in four long, lonely years, but staying now could only make it harder still.

'I'm not ready for this, Heath.' She blinked at him in the darkness, could still feel his warm breath on her cheek, the sting of his kiss on her lips. 'It's just not a good time right now.'

'Too much, too soon?'

She nodded, hating herself, because even that was a lie. There was no such thing as too much of Heath, and as for too soon—now that it had arrived, Bella felt as if she'd been waiting for ever.

'We'll take things slowly, then.' Tracing a finger along her jaw, he lifted her chin to look at him. 'Coffee will just be coffee. I want to get to know you a bit better, find out a bit about you. So far it's all been about me.'

'There's just too much going on in my life right now, Heath...'

'Then tell me about it,' he pushed, but, clinging to the steering-wheel for dear life, she shook her head.

'Please, Heath, just go.'

He didn't slam the door, wasn't anything other than the perfect gentleman as he got out and walked to his home, but as Bella drove off, she knew how much she'd hurt him, and knew that she'd completely confused him. He'd merely wanted to find out more about her, but that was the one thing she simply couldn't give.

Letting herself into her flat, she stared at the blinking green light of her answering-machine and balled her fists against her temples as the strained sound of Danny's mother's voice filled the air, Joyce urging her to call, wondering why she hadn't been in to see Danny this evening, and every word only lacerated Bella further. Every word turned the knife in her heart a notch more. Guilt layered upon guilt as it hit her that Danny lay helpless and alone in the nursing home and that after all these years, despite her vehement denials when it had first happened, she was doing what every person had said she one day would.

Moving on with her life.

CHAPTER SEVEN

'IT ISN'T enough, Bella.'

Detective Miller didn't look like a detective, Bella decided, staring over her coffee cup and trying to look as alert as one could at six a.m.

Which probably meant he was a good one, Bella mused. Dressed in jeans and a scruffy jumper, he looked like any other guy in any other café, chatting over coffee as he thickly buttered his toast.

'I know who it is,' Bella insisted. 'If I owned a house, I'd bet on it.'

'I'm with you.' Detective Miller shrugged. 'I don't doubt you're right, but at the end of the day, the evidence we've got won't stand up in court. We need something more solid if we want to get a conviction.'

'Like?'

'Caught red-handed springs to mind.'

'But I'm off after today. I'm not due back till Saturday night.'

'No chance of doing an extra shift?'

'I'd be happy to, but I've already been warned I'm doing too much. There's no way I can squeeze in another shift.'

'Even if Admin arranged it?'

Bella shook her head. 'It would look too suspicious. Who's going to watch the drugs while I'm not there?'

'Leave that for me to sort out, I'll have a word with the nursing coordinator. Hell, even if we have to get the drug room painted tomorrow by a couple of detectives, I'll make damn sure that cupboard's being watched.' He glanced down at his watch. 'You'd better get over there.' He gestured to the hospital over the road. 'If nothing goes down today, I'll see you at the station tomorrow. I'm due in court later on so I doubt we'll get a chance to meet up any time today—unless, of course, we get a result.' He stared down at her fingers drumming onto the table. 'Don't look so anxious, Bella.'

'This isn't anxious.' Bella gave a wry grin. 'This is just me.'

'Well, good luck. And one other thing, Bella.' Leaning over the table, he spoke in very low but very clear tones. 'Next time you decide to get up close and personal with a suspect, at least have the brains to think things through! You could have been sprung if Andy hadn't been on the ball.'

Mortified, Bella closed her eyes and buried her face in her hand for a moment before peering out between her fingers.

'I went for a drink. Emergency staff do it all the time. He didn't have a car, it would have looked strange if I'd—'

'I don't want excuses, Bella,' Detective Miller broke in. 'I just want you to be careful out there. This could still prove dangerous!'

'I know,' Bella gulped, suitably chastised and mentally kicking herself for her own stupidity last night. 'It won't happen again.'

'I never said you couldn't go for a drink with the staff. Hell, Bella, I want you to fit in, I want you to act as naturally as possible. But just be careful. Think things through before you act, that's all I'm saying.'

Handover was incredibly fast as Hannah was anxious to get home to take her husband to a hospital appointment and Jayne was keen to get the day started and hopefully squeeze in a bit of staff training along the way, but she took her time to explain carefully about the single patient in Resus, Darcy Mendleson, a nine-month-old presenting with a query febrile convulsion. Heath was in there and not quite happy with his own very tentative diagnosis, sure that the mother, despite gentle questioning and vehement denials, was covering something up.

'Have we rung DOCS?' Jayne asked, checking whether the Department of Community Services had been contacted— the first port of call when a suspicion of child abuse was raised. They were the ones who had to ask the difficult questions…

'Heath has.' Hannah nodded. 'They're going to send a team over, but I doubt it will be much before nine.'

'Right.' Jayne looked around at the assembled staff as Hannah gratefully scrambled away. 'Does anybody have any preferences where they go?'

Only Bella put up her hand. 'Could I do Resus again, please, Jayne?'

'Haven't you had enough yet?'

Lying through her teeth, Bella managed a 'no'. 'It's been good experience. I feel as if I'm almost up to date with all the new equipment.'

'Well, fine by me,' Jayne said briskly. 'But before you go, Bella, next time you have an issue with one of the ancillary staff, would you mind letting me deal with it instead of bawling them out in the corridor? We value our domestic staff in this department, they're as much a part of the team as the doctors and nurses are, and attempting to pull rank doesn't impress anyone.'

Cheeks burning, Bella managed a nod.

'Tony doesn't just have Emergency to clean, he's got the outpatients corridor and Pharmacy to deal with as well, so bear that in mind next time you need a box of tissues! He's also put his hand up for an extra shift on Saturday night because no one else wants to do it and, frankly, if that's how the domestic staff are spoken to, I'm not that surprised no one wants to work down here. Now, normally I'd be having this conversation behind closed doors in my office but, given that you chose to reprimand Tony in full view of any passer-by, I figured it wouldn't hurt to do it here. Not very nice, is it?'

Bella would have loved nothing more than to answer back, to tell Jayne exactly what she thought, but instead she had to swallow her pride and stammer out an apology, before heading off to check on her one single, very small patient before checking and rechecking all the equipment, wishing she was anywhere other than in the same room as Heath as he scribbled up some notes on the baby, the silence deafening, the atmosphere so appallingly tense you could have cut it with a knife.

'Have the paeds answered their pager yet, Sister?' Heath asked, clearly having decided things would be strictly professional between them, not even looking up as Bella checked the baby's vitals. As the wall phone trilled, she was saved from answering.

'They're stuck on the ward,' Heath sighed, hanging up the receiver and heading back to the babe. 'What are his obs doing?'

'His temp's still a bit on the high side—thirty-seven point nine.'

'That's what it was when he came in,' Heath said grimly. 'I'm not entirely happy this is a straightforward febrile convulsion. You'd expect his temperature to have been through the roof. I'm just not happy with him.'

Bella didn't like that voice, didn't like that slightly pensive shift when a very senior doctor looked at a seemingly stable patient.

Embarrassment and differences pushed aside, Bella looked at him properly for the first time since coming into the room.

'What do you think's going on?'

'I don't know,' Heath admitted. 'He's had a cold for a couple of days. Apart from that, he's been OK. Mum woke up at six this morning, heard him making a funny sound and found him convulsing. She called the paramedics but he'd stopped fitting by the time they got there and was crying.' He was relaying the story as much for his own benefit as hers, going over and over the puzzle of diagnosis to see if anything had been missed.

'Any more convulsions?' Bella asked, and Heath shook his head.

'He was slightly drowsy on arrival but still appropriate for a nine-month-old. After that he fell asleep, which is normal after a fit. His ears are a bit pink, throat's clear, bloods all pretty normal.'

'So what doesn't sit right?'

'His temperature for starters, though I guess he could have cooled down by the time he got here. But febrile convulsion patients are normally flushed and irritable...' He stared down at the baby, picking up a little fat hand as he did so and holding it.

'There's not a mark on him.'

'Are you thinking this could be non-accidental?'

'I'm starting to,' Heath admitted. 'It just doesn't add up.'

'Where's Mum?'

'Ringing her boyfriend. He'd just left for work when all this happened. He delivers for the local baker or something. She's having a hell of a time getting hold of him.'

'So this all happened after he left for work?'

Heath nodded then grimly headed for the telephone. 'I'm going to try and organize a head CT, though I don't fancy my chances.'

His hunch proved right.

'They're backed up.'

'Already?'

'The neuro ward's got a patient in there and ICU's got one waiting. A conscious baby and a doctor with a hunch isn't going to hurry things along.'

'Speak to the mum,' Bella urged.

'I already have.' Heath ran an exasperated hand through his hair. 'I can't just confront her, not without going through the proper channels. I'll ring DOCS.'

'Which will take for ever,' Bella needlessly pointed out.

'I can't just wade in and accuse her. It isn't done like that any more. And without the Department of Community Services or the police, I'm not even supposed to mention it.'

'How is he?' A thin, nervous-looking woman entered Resus, anxious eyes swinging between Bella and Heath, her face pale apart from a splash of lipstick and some crudely applied blusher.

'Hi, Rose,' Heath answered as Bella's eyes took in every flicker of the woman's reaction. 'He's much the same.'

'That's good, isn't it?'

'Not necessarily.' Bella's voice had a slightly shrill ring to it and she was vaguely aware of Heath tensing beside her, clearly un-used to any nurse speaking in such a way, but her eyes were firmly on Darcy's mother. 'We need you to go through the morning's events again.'

'I've already explained what happened,' Rose answered, walking over to the cot and taking her baby's hand. 'I've told the doctor.'

'It's important that we go through it again,' Bella responded, 'just in case we've missed something.'

'I've told you everything. Keith left for work, I was half-awake, I suppose, when I heard a sound.'

'What sort of sound?' Bella checked.

'A cry.' Rose shrugged. 'A wail. I just knew it didn't sound right.'

'So what did you do?'

'I went in.' Rose's eyes were brimming with tears. 'Do I really have to go through all this again?'

'Could I have a word, Sister?' Heath's request left absolutely no room for negotiation and Bella had no choice but to excuse herself and step outside. The livid face that greeted her wasn't exactly welcoming. 'Just what the hell do you think you're doing in there?'

'I'm trying to find out what happened,' Bella answered hotly.

'Not like that, Bella. You don't just wade in and practically accuse someone.' Heath's voice had a warning note but Bella couldn't have cared less.

'She's hiding something and you know it as well as I do. If we wait, if we go through the so-called correct channels, then that little baby could end up with brain damage if he hasn't already got it.'

'Do you think I don't know that?' Heath responded. 'Do you think I don't want to go in there and demand the truth? But we can't, Bella.'

'Just watch me.' Bella glared. 'Or wait outside, if you have to. The fact of the matter is that unless we get to the bottom of this quickly, that baby could be in serious trouble, and if my nursing registration is the price I pay then so be it.'

And if she sounded like a bitch, she didn't care. Four years on the police force had hardened her enough and this softly-softly approach had gone on long enough. She'd told Detective Miller that she wouldn't compromise patient care and she had meant it.

'OK, Rose.' Bella was straight back into the cubicle, aware of Heath walking in behind her. 'What happened after you heard him cry?'

'I went in to him. He was shaking, having a fit or something, and I called the ambulance.' She swung her eyes to Heath in a silent plea for help. 'I don't know what she's trying to get at, but I'm telling you the truth.'

'That's all we want, Rose,' Bella answered calmly, ignoring Heath's uncomfortable stance and pushing on regardless. 'Because if you're missing anything out then now really is the time to tell us.'

'I'm telling you the truth,' Rose said.

'Enough, Bella,' Heath broke in, shooting her a warning look before addressing the shaking mother. 'Rose, our concern is that Darcy doesn't quite fit the picture of a febrile convulsion. Now, ideally I'd like to send him for an urgent CT scan, but at the moment his symptoms don't warrant it and there are patients apparently sicker than Darcy waiting. But if he does have a head injury, if something's happened that you're not telling us, we could move things along faster. It's imperative that you tell us everything. Every detail's important no matter how small it might seem to you. We're just trying to get a clear picture here of what exactly happened this morning.'

'I've told you,' Rose sobbed. 'I've told you everything that's happened.'

'Not quite,' Bella said softly, but her voice was firm, her sharp eyes scanning the woman's face, watching the color mount in her cheeks as Bella spoke on, voicing the first thing that had sprung to her mind when the woman had entered the room. 'You haven't told us when you got a chance to put your lipstick on, Rose. You haven't told us when during all this unfolding drama you had the time to put on some blusher.'

There was no joy in being proved right as Rose visibly crumpled, no surge of triumph as Bella's instincts were proved correct. Staring at the baby lying in the cot, Bella would have been more than happy to have got it all wrong.

'What happened, Rose?' Bella said, but more gently now. 'For Darcy's sake we really need to know.'

'He's been crying and miserable for two days with this cold,' Rose sobbed. 'Keith was exhausted. He gets up at five, he needs his sleep. He just lost it, only for a moment, though...'

She could see Heath's knuckles turn white as he held on to the cot side, his face set in stone as Rose spoke on.

'He just shook him, only for a moment.'

'When?'

'Two, three a.m. I'm not sure, he didn't hit him or anything. Darcy wasn't even crying.'

'And then what?' Bella pushed as Heath headed for the phone.

'He went to sleep. I watched him all night. I decided once Keith went to work I'd get Darcy bathed and dressed and take him to my GP to get him checked out, but he started shaking...'

'We can take him straight round.' Heath came over. 'CT will take him now. I'm going to go with him. Could you set up some equipment for me in case I need to intubate?' He was pulling up anticonvulsant drugs in case he might need them, things moving more

quickly now that the diagnosis had undoubtedly shifted.

'He'll be OK?' Rose begged.

'I don't know,' Heath admitted. 'Shaking
babies can cause serious damage. Their heads
are large in comparison to their bodies,
they've got little neck control, and a number
of injuries could have occurred, but you did
the right thing, telling us.'

'She did nothing right,' Bella snarled a couple of hours later, choking back tears as
Heath came into the staffroom. She was gulp-
ing a coffee so hot it scalded her throat. 'She
lied through her teeth to save herself.'

'What if she hadn't been?' Heath answered
equally brutally. 'You were way out of line
in there.'

'I got her to tell the truth.'

'There are channels,' Heath barked. 'Pro-
cedures…'

'Oh, and you always stick by them?' Bella
hurled, emotions bubbling now. 'If I hadn't

spoken the way I did we'd still be waiting for DOCS to arrive, we'd still be sitting on our hands, tied by red tape and getting nowhere.'

'I don't understand you, Bella,' Heath rasped. 'One minute you're warm and loving and full of empathy and the next…' His jaw clenched as he bit back spiteful words. His voice was measured when finally he continued, 'As much as we don't condone what Rose did, she isn't the guilty one here. It was her boyfriend who did this…'

'While she sat back and watched.'

'You know, I'm glad things didn't go further last night.' Heath stared at her with sheer disbelief on his face. 'Because I'm starting to realize that there's a hard side to you, Bella, that I don't think I like very much.'

'She lied,' Bella insisted, but the phone ringing halted her tirade. 'If that's DOCS, tell them the baby's up on Intensive Care with a detached retina and a bleed in his brain. If Rose had only told the truth when she got here…'

Picking up the phone, his face was grim. He listened to the message before covering the receiver and holding it out to her.

'Speaking of the truth...' He shot a thinly disguised look of loathing. 'It's your fiancé's parents on the phone for you.'

'Heath, please,' Bella started, but the shutters were already down, and handing her the phone he walked out without a single word.

'Think it through.'

That was what Detective Miller had said and that was what she did. Somehow surviving the shift, watching like a hawk colleagues who were fast becoming friends, sharing in the dramas and quiet moments of Emergency and feeling like the worst woman in the world.

She had to tell him.

That was all Bella knew, the only thought that kept her going as she somehow ploughed through the day. Not everything, of course, but at least about Danny, tell him how somewhere along the way she'd lost that little piece inside that was a prerequisite in nursing.

'Can we talk?' Beth asked hours later, when her shift should have been long since over and the back-up in the waiting room had long since gone.

'I don't think there's much to say, do you?' Heath clipped, sitting at the empty nurses' station staring at the patient folder in front of him, even though it was blank. 'If there's something on your mind, Bella, shouldn't it be your fiancé you're talking to?'

'I talk to him nearly every day.' There was a wobble in her voice that had him turning, watching as this proud chameleon woman took a tiny step down from the distant pedestal that, despite her apparent openness, she somehow always managed to cling to. 'The trouble is, he doesn't hear me.'

'That's not my problem, Bella,' Heath responded, balling his fist to stop him reaching out, his words coming out way too harsh through his clenched jaw. 'You should be saying this to him, not me.'

'I can't,' Bella admitted, watching as he shook his head in exasperation. 'I can't because Danny's in a nursing home. He's been there for four years and no matter how I try I can't quite bring myself to say that I can't do this any more.' Heath's devastated expression, the utter sympathy blazing in his eyes wasn't helping. 'And you were completely right with what you said before— there is a hard side to me that probably doesn't belong in an emergency room because I can't stand by and beat around the bush, treat someone with kid gloves just because protocol demands it.'

'There have to be rules, Bella,' Heath said, but far more gently now. 'If we'd accused her and been wrong, what sort of damage could we have done?'

'What about the damage they've done?' Bella responded, her voice quiet but thick with emotion. 'I know better than anyone the long-term devastation a serious head injury causes, and I couldn't just sit back and watch that baby get worse while we waited for DOCS to arrive. If Danny had been treated promptly when he first arrived in Emergency there's no doubt in my mind that he'd be walking around today instead of sitting in a geriatric nursing home because there's no-where else to put him.'

'Was he brought here?' Heath asked, and Bella shook her head.

'He came to my hospital...' And she couldn't do it any more, couldn't stand and relive the agony with the sickening smell of antiseptic in the air, the overhead Tannoy crackling overhead, the sounds and smells too brutal right now, too reminiscent of the worst day of her life.

'I can't do this,' she gasped, shaking off his hand as he reached out to her, choking back tears that had never really been shed. 'I should just go home...'

'I'll take you home,' Heath said firmly. 'I'm supposed to be finished anyway.'

'No.' She shook her head because even though it was what she wanted, even though the chance to open up to someone, to reveal, to share was something she needed so badly right now, she still had to lie. Couldn't take the man she wanted to be with now into a home filled with photos, her uniform, an answering-machine bleeping with urgent messages, piles of security tape, the blazing evidence of a part of her he didn't even know existed. But she needed Heath, needed him like she'd never needed anyone before. 'I don't want to go there.'

'How about that coffee at mine, then?' Heath asked softly, but in his own teasing way he still had to have the last word. 'You could have done all this yesterday, Bella.'

CHAPTER EIGHT

INCREDIBLY shy, Bella walked into Heath's home, and even though the furnishings were supremely male—dark leather couches, a massive plasma screen TV and enough stereo equipment to land a Boeing 747—the place was incredibly clean and tidy.

'Good-looking *and* tidy.' Bella smiled, attempting to break the awkward silence, neither of them so assured now away from the safety of the hospital.

'Only because I'm never here.' Heath shrugged. 'Though come this time next week, the place will look as if a bomb's hit it.' He gestured to a collection of photos on top of a very ordered bookcase and Bella wandered over, picking up a heavy wooden frame and staring down into the green eyes of two gorgeous blond children, gappy smiles grinning back at her.

'These are very nice skeletons to have in your wardrobe,' Bella said, more than happy not to talk about herself for a while. 'How old are they?'

'Max is seven, and Lily's six, or at least that's what her birth certificate says. I swear she's more knowing than most adults.'

'It must have hurt,' Bella said, replacing the photo carefully and seeing the pain in his face when he nodded slowly.

'I was devastated,' Heath openly admitted. 'It felt at the time as if I was losing everything, so I came out fighting, did the stupid macho thing and got some hot-shot solicitor, told her she'd have to fight for every cent, demanded that I have full custody. I was a complete bastard actually, not just to Jackie but to everyone around me, hell-bent on making everyone as miserable as I was.'

'So what happened?'

'I finally grew up! And do you know the stupid part of it all was that once I calmed down I actually realized that Jackie had been right to leave, that we hadn't really been happy, that the hours I put in at work weren't all completely merited. She's so much happier now, and the kids are great.'

'And you see them a lot?'

'All the time.' Heath grinned. 'Every other weekend plus a day or two during the other week—more than I did when I was married, actually.'

'And how are things with you and Jackie?'

'Getting there!' Heath rolled his eyes and even managed to make her laugh a little bit as he pulled a face. 'We're working hard on being friends.'

Selecting a bottle from the wine rack, Bella sat nervously on the edge of the massive sofa, glad of the tiny reprieve his back gave her as he uncorked a bottle of red, listening to the thick glugging sound as he poured two glasses, then handing one to her as he sat down beside her.

'You weren't on duty?' Heath asked, resuming the conversation where they'd left it at work.

'Unfortunately, no. I was at my flat, waiting for him to come over. We were going to go out for dinner, he was going to ask me to marry him…' Her hands were fidgeting in her lap. Heath's closed around them and she clung on gratefully. 'I wasn't supposed to know, of course, but he'd asked my dad, who'd told my mum, who—'

'Had to tell you?' Heath said gently, and Bella nodded.

'So there I was, dressed up to the nines, waiting for him to come over. Apparently he'd got the ring and had stopped at a bar to show his friend. He only had one drink, but he bought a bottle of champagne, I think it must have been for us to have later. Anyway, there I was, waiting for him to come over, when I got this phone call.' Tears were falling and she didn't even bother to wipe them, just clutched his hands and tried to summon the strength to carry on.

'The hospital?' Heath pushed gently.

'Danny,' Bella corrected. 'He was in the waiting room. He told me he'd been bashed, that he was waiting to be seen and that the staff thought he was drunk, but he'd only had one. He stank of alcohol because his attacker cracked his skull with a full champagne bottle, but I didn't know that!' Closing her eyes, she willed her voice calm, could feel the hysteria creeping in as she relived her awful tale. 'His voice was all slurred, he sounded terrible, he said he had this headache and that no one was listening to him. He was getting hysterical, shouting and crying into the phone and asking me what to do.'

'So what did you do?'

'The wrong thing,' Bella gulped. 'I should have rung the hospital, told them it was my boyfriend, told them that he had to be seen straight away, but instead I jumped in the car.

I thought I could sort it out when I got there, I thought that maybe they were right, maybe he had been drinking.'

'Bella you couldn't have known. This isn't your fault.'

'I know that,' Bella gulped. 'Deep down I know that, but *they* should have known, they should have seen the state he was in, at least done a decent set of obs and observed him. I couldn't find him when I got there and they thought at first he'd walked out, but he was in the toilet, Heath, lying in the toilet cubicle, not even breathing when they found him.'

'Oh, Bella.' He didn't even try to stay objective or impartial, didn't even try to keep the appalling regret out of his voice.

'You know how you called it on Andrew?' Her teeth were chattering, barely able to get the words out. 'Knew that getting him back wasn't going to help anyone at all? Well, Danny didn't even get that. By then they knew they'd seriously messed up, so they panicked, worked on him for a long time when they should have just stopped, just kept going and going till somehow they got him back.'

'Hell.' Heath shook his head. 'What a mess. It must have been hell.'

'It still is hell!' Angry eyes stared back at him. 'Hell for everyone involved. The staff involved, Danny's parents, me, but most of all for Danny. Danny was the most fun-loving, fittest guy I've ever known. He loved surfing, played lots of footy, you could barely contain him indoors. He was always dressed in shorts and a T-shirt.' She shook her head hopelessly. 'I'd never seen him in a suit until I arrived at the hospital, he'd gone and bought one so he'd look smart when he proposed to me. He'd even had his hair cut—I was always nagging him about it. But if you see him now, Heath, he's just an empty shell, and his parents are still dragging it through the courts, still hoping he's going to come round. And it just won't end, it just won't ever end.'

'Do you still see him?'

'Nearly every day,' Bella said. 'How do I stop? How do I say that I can't do this any more, that I want to go on with my life, when every time I miss a visit his parents ring, every time I take a step forward, try to move on, they remind me we were engaged.'

'About to be engaged,' Heath corrected, but Bella gave an exhausted shrug.

'We would have been engaged,' Bella said with complete certainty. 'We'd have been married now and probably had a couple of kids. Part of me knows I have to move on, but part of me says that surely it's wrong...'

'What would Danny want for you?' Heath tried, and when she didn't respond he tried a different tack. 'If it had happened to you, what would you want Danny to do?' But Bella just let out a weary, mirthless laugh.

'I've tried that one, Heath, and maybe I'm just plain selfish, but the last thing I'd want is to be forgotten, the last thing I'd want is to be sitting trapped in a nursing home while everyone else got on with their life. I just don't know what to do, I just can't see any way out.'

'It doesn't have to be black and white, Bella. Just because you move on with your life, it doesn't mean you have to cut Danny out completely.'

'You don't understand.'

'Oh, yes, I do, Bella. You're scared of the confrontation, scared of admitting it to Danny's parents when you're not even sure you're ready to admit it yourself that it's time to start living your life again. And maybe they won't understand, maybe they'll never come around because at the end of the day he's their son, but it doesn't mean you have to compromise yourself, you can still do what's right for you. You can still see Danny, still go in, but instead of every day maybe make it once a week or once a month. You can still be there for him, but it doesn't have to mean it's at the exclusion of everyone else.

You are allowed to have other relationships, Bella.'

'Perhaps.' She gave a hopeless shrug. 'But tell me, Heath, what sort of guy would put up with all that? What sort of man would put up with his girlfriend going in to visit her ex-fiancé once a week?'

'This one,' Heath said firmly. 'If you can put up with my ex-wife, I can put up with your ex-fiancé.' He saw her wince at the final word, shake her head at the impossibility of it all.

'It's too soon to be talking like this.' Pulling her hands away, she angrily wiped her cheeks. 'This is all just going way too fast. We've only known each other a few days.'

'So?' Heath seemed completely unfazed by her response. 'I know how I feel, Bella, and I think you do, too. Yes, it's been a bit fast and, yes, it probably doesn't all make sense, but it doesn't change the—'

'We don't even know each other,' Bella argued, barely able to comprehend that he felt it, too, that this delicious man in front of her adored her as much as she did him, and it was the scariest confrontation of her life. 'We haven't even slept together…'

'Well, we can soon take care of that.'

Lips that had been on hers only yesterday were moving back where they belonged and Bella ached to lean towards him, to catch just a little of the strength and hope he had for them both, lean on him for a moment, feel the weight of his kiss, the bliss of being held, after so many long lonely years.

'I'm scared, Heath.'

'I know.' His words were muffled in her hair, his arms wrapping tightly around her and holding her close. 'But you have nothing to be afraid of. We don't have to do anything that you don't want to.'

'But I do want to.' Blinking into his chest, she breathed the words, scarcely able to believe her own boldness. She could feel his heart hammering in his chest, smell the delectable scent of him, and even if her feelings terrified her, even if this was the most reckless, scariest thing she'd ever done in her life, there was no place Bella wanted to be other than in his arms. 'I'm just...' Swallowing hard, she closed her eyes, embarrassed to admit the truth, unsure of his reaction. 'Heath, it's been so long. I don't want to let you down...'

'Hey.' Pulling back slightly, he smiled down at her. 'How could you even begin to let me down when this is about both of us, Bella? It's up to both of us to make this work.' And there was something infinitely reassuring about the eyes that held hers, something deeper going on than basic lust, a coming home almost. And when he stood and offered her his hand, without hesitation she took it, letting him lead her up the stairs and into his bedroom, standing shy but not awkward as he slowly undressed her, yielding under his gentle touch. Undressing was supposed to be awkward but not with Heath. Every button was gently undone as if he were opening a deliciously wrapped parcel, thick, firm finger wedging into the waistband of her skirt, gliding down the zipper and capturing her buttocks as he slid her panties and skirt down, tiny moans of pleasure escaping his lips as he kissed her swollen breasts. And such was his approval, such was his blatant admiration, it made her bolder still, gave her the courage she needed to unwrap a parcel of her own, trembling fingers working the buttons of his shirt then burying her lips in the satin skin of his torso. He tasted divine, the tangy salty taste of his chest beneath her lips, fingers tracing the blond hair that fed like a tiny whirlpool around his nipples. Her hand bolder now, pressing the flesh beneath her, a delicious Braille beneath her fingers as she followed the path down to its delicious end, capturing him swollen and glorious in her hands. She almost wept at the emotions he unleashed, the primitive need he had somehow ignited in her again, remembering yet somehow forgetting at the same time just how right it was to be held, touched, embraced with love.

Gently he laid her down then joined her, side by side on the pillow, and with eyes wide open she stared back, nerves catching up as his fingers became more insistent, probing her most sensitive place. She wrestled for a second, contrary feelings washing over her, the sensible part of her mind telling her to push him away, to somehow save herself from the exposure this could surely bring. But still he was holding her, still his hands were loving her, and Bella felt herself relent, felt the delicious flood of earthy arousal somewhere deep inside, nerves forgotten as need took over, her groin moving in his hand, her thighs gently parted, needing more, needing him to fill her. Heath understood, slipping inside her with a thrust that was urgent, filling her over and over, the delicious friction of man and woman moving in tune, one hand pushing her buttocks as the other held the back of her head. And she needed his hand there, needed him to steady her as her neck arched backwards, as a distant pulse drew nearer, her whole body spasming in delicious abandonment, dragging him in ever deeper, feeling the delicious swell of his come inside her, the low throaty moan as he buried his face in her shoulder, the thrilling chill of his tongue as he drew back and kissed her tenderly.

Tears stung in Bella's eyes at the sheer release of it all, the tense knot inside he had freed, the utter absence of regret or guilt as the world started to trickle in. Heath was totally unfazed by her tears, understanding in an instant how hard it had been for her to finally let go. Rolling onto his back, he pulled her head down to his chest, holding her close in silent understanding, gently stroking her hair till the tears abated and sleep washed over them.

CHAPTER NINE

'GO BACK to sleep.' Heath grinned as Bella blinked her swollen eyes open. 'You're off duty today.' She stared up at him, utterly divine in a sharp suit with a tie haphazardly knotted, hair wet from the shower, running an electric razor over his chin and clearly very late for work, but not in that much of a hurry that he didn't register the flicker of guilt in her eyes, the nervous swallow as she took in her surroundings.

Sitting down on the bed, he captured her thigh through the sheet, but the gesture was more reassuring than sexy. 'It's OK to be happy, Bella.'

'I know,' she said, not sounding entirely convinced then giving it a second go. 'I know it is. Heath?' Tense eyes avoided him. 'But how am I going to tell Danny's parents? They're never going to forgive me.'

'It isn't going to be easy telling them,' Heath agreed gently.

'They still think that one day he's going to somehow magically be OK. That he's going to suddenly start talking and walking, that he's going to come back to them and that we'll take up where we left off. They're both so positive, which should be good...'

'Not when there isn't any hope,' Heath broke in, and she was grateful for his honesty, glad to be able to discuss this most difficult subject with someone who really seemed to understand.

'It's going to be so horridly awkward telling them, but it isn't me that I'm worried about. Well, a bit,' Bella admitted. 'But it's more the fact I've met someone else, that I'm moving on. It is just going to upset them.'

'Have you ever considered that it might just help?' Heath asked. 'Not straight away, of course, but this might be the wake-up call they need to realize that Danny isn't ever going to get any better.'

'Perhaps,' Bella sighed. 'But I just hate being the one to extinguish their last ray of hope.' Closing her eyes for a moment, Bella dwelt on the problem, knowing deep down what she had to do yet dreading it all the same. 'Before I speak to Joyce and Joe, I have to tell Danny first. He deserves that at least, though I don't think for a moment that he'll understand what I'm saying.'

'You tell him when you're ready,' Heath said gently. 'There's no rush, Bella. I'm not going to demand that you go down there and tell him tonight, for heaven's sake. Things have happened so quickly between us, it's no wonder you're confused. Maybe you should get it straight in your own head before you tell him,' he suggested, but Bella shook her head.

'I can't see you without him knowing, it would feel as if I were...'

'Cheating?' Heath suggested.

Bella nodded. Pulling at a tendril of hair, she wrapped it round and round her fingers as she spoke, fidgeting just as she always did when she was nervous. 'He turns thirty in a couple of weeks, his parents have been planning this party for ages. Some music and balloons at his bedside, they've bought him a gold chain...' Her voice wavered, the full horror of telling them starting to hit home. 'I just don't want to ruin that day for them...'

'That's fine,' Heath said easily.

'I'm not avoiding anything,' Bella argued needlessly. 'But I won't be able to see much of you for a couple of weeks. I don't think that would be fair to them or Danny, but I'll make it up to you. I just need to do this one thing for them. You're right, I need to get it straight in my own head before I tell them.'

'That's fine,' Heath said again, and this time she managed to look at him. His green eyes were smiling back at her, that gorgeous smile still there, completely and utterly com-

fortable whatever her decision. Maybe he
was right, maybe it really was fine.

'You understand?'

'I don't have to,' Heath answered, and it
confused her. 'If I've learnt one thing, Bella,
it's that relationships that really work aren't
all about give and take and compromise and
not having to explain every last move.
Relationships are about acceptance. And if
holding off telling Danny's parents is what's
right for you, then that's good enough. You
don't have to justify yourself to me, Bella,
you don't have to make it up to me, the same
way I hope I never have to make it up to you
if one of the kids are sick and I have to go
over, or Jackie decides we need to sit down
and talk and I'm half an hour late coming
home.'

'Coming home?'

'We both know where this is leading.'
Heath stared at her unwaveringly. 'I've
known since the second I looked up and saw
you standing outside Resus, Bella.'

And it was scary and huge yet completely true. From the second Bella had laid eyes on him she'd been filled with something precious, something exhilarating and exciting. And as utterly indefinable as it was, it was real.

'We've both got pasts, Bella. Both got people in our lives who really matter to us, and if we can't deal with that then there's no point even trying.'

She'd never heard such utter confidence, the kind of certainty, and inner strength she could only aspire to.

'You've really got your head together, haven't you?'

'Finally.' Heath grinned. 'Though it took a while.'

'Don't you ever check your messages?' Detective Miller growled as Bella walked into the meeting room late on Saturday afternoon, an easy smile in place and for once not fidgeting as she sat down with her colleagues.

Maybe Heath's inner confidence was infectious, Bella decided, because instead of blabbing out a stream of excuses, instead of fidgeting with her hair, she gave a tiny shrug. 'I've been trying to get hold of you all day.'

'Even I'm allowed some time off, Detective Miller,' Bella answered with a smile.

'Hell, you're even starting to sound like a detective now!'

'Right, Phil, what have we got?'

'A migraine,' he moaned, sitting and scowling in paint-splattered overalls. 'What do you expect, tucked in that little room, smelling paint fumes all day?'

'Nothing amiss?'

'Nothing. The drugs are still there.'

'Bella?'

'Still sticking with my theory,' Bella replied confidently.

'It's still only a theory,' he pointed out, shaking his head as Bella attempted to argue.

'I'm not jeopardizing all this work on a uniformed constable's hunch.'

'Thanks for the vote of confidence,' Bella complained, but she wasn't remotely offended. Compliments were rare at the best of times in this line of work and markedly absent prior to a result.

'Look, guys, we've put in too many man hours, too much time to blow it now. Yes, I agree with Bella. We think we know who's doing it, but we still don't know how. So I've decided that this has gone on long enough and needs to be hurried along. It's about time we find out.' He glanced at his watch. 'Right about now, Pharmacy's going to deliver a bigger stock of morphine than usual.'

'On what pretext?' Bella asked, frowning.

'Apparently they used a lot on Sunday night. There's nothing untoward in that, though, all the charts have been checked...'

'There were a lot of cardiac patients when I came on duty,' Bella agreed.

'Well, they're going to deliver five boxes of morphine and if anyone questions it, the pharmacist is going to give some excuse about the computer averages or something and that it will all be corrected with next week's stocktake. He seemed to think that would sound OK.' Bella nodded. As always, Detective Miller was right. His well-laid plans, as always, completely spot on, and Bella was filled with admiration for her temporary boss, hoping, not for the first time, that her position might become permanent, while knowing that for it to happen she had to get this right. Tonight things had to go her way. 'So with all our suspects on duty tonight and five tempting boxes, let's hope for all our sakes we get a result.'

With an end possibly in sight, Bella's newly acquired confidence was diminishing rapidly. Her mind whirred as she made her way to work, going over and over her own mental notes, checking and rechecking her theory just to be sure she was right. And as much as she'd have loved to have dwelt on the thought of seeing Heath at work later, tonight was just too big for any diversions, no matter how appealing. But she allowed herself one tiny luxurious glimpse, one grateful sigh that hopefully soon this would all be over, that soon she'd be able to tell Heath the whole truth, and hopefully he'd be as understanding about her police work as he had been about Danny, hopeful then she could really start life over again.

'Ready for some real work?' Hannah asked, as Bella joined her outside in the courtyard, grabbing a quick coffee before the clock edged to nine.

'Typical night staff.' Bella grinned. 'Always assuming that they're busier than everyone else.'

'It's a fact,' Hannah moaned. 'I've got the varicose veins to prove it. Who ever said nursing was sexy wants shooting!' Rolling up her trouser legs, she gave Bella a glimpse of the network of blue veins on her calf and both women started to laugh. 'Lucky for me Ken's eyesight's fading. He still thinks I'm gorgeous.'

'You are.' Bella grinned. 'And possibly just a bit mad as well.' Glancing down at her watch, she let out a long sigh. 'I guess we'd better get out there.'

'You go, I'm going to finish my coffee first and wrap up Jim's leaving present, then I'd better lock it in the drug cupboard. The last thing we want going missing is that!' Hannah waved her off. 'And if Jayne asks, say that you haven't seen me. I'm sick of her moods lately. She used to be the most laid-back of us all.'

'It must be hard, being in charge,' Bella suggested, but Hannah just gave a dismissive snort.

'Oh, I'd take the grief for the wages they're paying her and I'd manage a smile at the same time.'

*   *   *

'Nice day off?' Heath asked as Bella joined the group at the desk to await handover.

'Very.' Bella smiled, sharing in one indulgent moment before pulling out her pad and getting ready to start.

'Can I have someone to check the drugs?' one of the day staff asked, shaking her head as one of the junior nurses put up her hand. 'Better have one of the seniors.' She rolled her eyes heavenwards. 'Pharmacy's only gone and messed up and given us five boxes of morphine. They're going to sort it with next week's order, but given the current state of affairs…'

'Say no more,' Jayne groaned, dumping her bag under the desk, no doubt meaning to lock it up later. 'OK. I'll come and check them. Handover will just have to wait. Where's Hannah, by the way?'

'I've no idea,' Bella answered, her eyes drifting beyond Jayne as the waiting-room doors slid open and a patient was brought through in a wheelchair by Jim the porter, catching sight of Detective Miller, jeans and scruffy jumper firmly in place, blending in perfectly with the rest of the waiting room as he chatted easily to yet another of Bella's undercover colleagues. But the fact he was here added another notch of pressure to Bella's shoulders, the weight of expectation firmly in place.

'What have I missed?' Hannah asked, sidling up beside Bella.

'Nothing. Jayne's gone to check the drugs. Apparently Pharmacy's messed up and sent five boxes of morphine by mistake.'

'Which was very sensible of them.' Hannah rolled her eyes sarcastically. 'I just hope to God they're still there in the morning, for all our sakes. I'll just go and give this to Jayne and ask her to lock it up.'

And because Bella wanted it to be busy, because she wanted the drug cupboard to be in constant use as it often was on a Saturday night, it was unusually quiet. The waiting room was full but, apart from a couple of abdominal pains and a child with asthma, most of the patients were suffering only minor complaints. By eleven o'clock Bella's nerves were in shreds, her whole body taut with nervous expectation, jumping a mile when Heath came up behind her as she sat on a stool, filling out a ward transfers slip for one of their few patients.

'Can I have some pethidine for cubicle five? I've tried Buscopan and it hasn't helped her abdominal pain.'

'Sure.' Almost grabbing the card from his hand, Bella jumped down, casting her eyes around for a nurse to come with her.

'It's not that urgent.' Heath grinned. 'You're very jumpy tonight.'

'It's the company I'm keeping.' Bella attempted a casual smile. 'I don't normally make a habit of sleeping with the boss.'

'Well, you do from now on,' Heath said, and something inside her melted on the spot. 'Do you want me to come and check it with you?'

'Check what?' Jayne asked, coming over and peering over Bella's shoulder. 'I'll do it. Heath, can you have another listen to that child's chest? He's had two Ventolin nebulizers but he's still very wheezy. I think we're going to end up admitting him, so we might as well get Paeds down now.'

'Where's Hannah?' Jayne frowned as Heath made his way over to the child sitting wheezing and miserable in the cubicle opposite.

'Cleaning up the staffroom,' Bella answered, trying desperately to keep the rather pained note out of her voice, remembering the dressing-down Jayne had given her when she'd pulled up Tony for his apparent lack of cleaning skills. 'Before she sets up for Jim's leaving do.'

They were at the drug room now, and Bella could feel her breath bursting in her lungs as they made their way in. She tried desperately to keep up the light-hearted chatter as Jayne unlocked the controlled drugs cupboard and flipped out the book, but her expression changed when she saw a neatly wrapped parcel, pulling it out and turning it over in her hands.

'What on earth's this?'

'Jim's gift,' Bella ventured. 'Hannah said she was going to ask you to lock it up for her.'

'Did she now?' Jayne shrugged, replacing the present and getting on with the checking, and Bella found herself frowning, positive Hannah had told her she would be giving the watch to Jayne to lock up. 'Pethidine, 50 milligrams.' Jayne started pulling open the box, going through the routine they both knew so well. But even though Bella checked the contents carefully, her eyes darted inside the cupboard, curiously deflated when everything appeared in order. The five boxes of morphine still sat neatly on the shelf. Everything was just as it should be, Jim's present neatly wrapped and tied with a bow, not a single thing out of place. 'Right, we'll give this and then, if you don't mind, can you go and help Hannah to set up the staffroom?' Jayne asked, pulling out the present and handing it to Bella. 'We might as well take advantage while the department's so quiet and give Jim his present now. Who knows what might come in later?'

Hannah had done an amazing job in such a short time, the sink for once free of cups, a massive handmade banner hanging on the wall, wishing Jim every luck for his retirement.

'You've been busy.' Bella smiled, taking a couple of peanuts from the table Hannah had laid, then opening the staff fridge and pulling out a box.

'I bought a cake.'

'Oh, you didn't have to do that,' Hannah tutted. 'You've only been here a week.'

'I've met a few Jims in my time, though,' Bella said fondly. 'I'm sure he more than deserves it. Is there anything I can do to help?'

'Round up the staff, I guess,' Hannah said excitedly, eyeing her handiwork. 'I'll go and ask Jayne to get the present.'

'She already gave it to me.' Bella pulled it out of her pocket, trying to keep her voice even as she added, hopefully lightly, 'I thought you said that Jayne had locked it up for you?'

'She did,' Hannah said absent-mindedly, cutting the cake into generous slices. 'Why?'

'She just seemed surprised to see it, that's all. As if she didn't even know it was in there.'

'Then she's losing her mind.' Hannah gave Bella a queer look as she took the precious parcel. 'I hope that Jim likes it. I took for ever to choose it.'

'I'm sure he will.'

Jim didn't just like it, he loved it. Tears filled his eyes as he unwrapped the little parcel, pulling out a beautiful watch and holding it fondly.

'Turn it over.' Hannah beamed, and everyone stood silent as Jim read the inscription.

'I'll miss you all, too,' he said in a voice thick with emotion. 'No doubt more than you'll miss me.'

'Rubbish,' everyone called, raising their glasses, but the noise died down as Heath made his way over, coming to stand beside Jim and addressing the gathered crowd.

'I started here ten years ago, and I know it's probably hard to believe but I wasn't nearly as good-looking or confident then.' A few more catcalls and giggles, before his voice grew more serious. 'Jim was on the first night I worked, and in those days there wasn't a consultant or registrar in the department, just me on my lonesome, and I don't mind telling you I was bloody terrified. All night Jim came up to me—"Are you going to take those bloods soon, Doctor? Only I'm on my way to the lab," or "Did you want that child to have another nebulizer before I take her round for her chest X-ray?" And it wasn't until about five in the morning when I was sitting smugly nursing my cup of tea and realizing I'd got through my first night alone without killing anyone, feeling pretty pleased with myself how I'd run the show, that I realized it hadn't been me running the show at all. Instead, it was this guy.' He held out a hand to Jim and shook his warmly. 'A guy who'd already been here for thirty years by then, who'd seen the first patient wheeled through the doors when the department opened. A guy who in his own quiet, unassuming way has helped all of us through our first nights. And you're wrong, Jim, to suggest you won't be missed. Everyone in this room is going to miss you, but it's not just us who are going to miss you, it's the new staff who start from here on who won't have you to guide them and the patients who won't have the benefit of your wisdom.'

And even though Bella had never worked with Jim, just seen him going off duty a few times, she could feel her own eyes filling as

Heath delivered his lovely speech, knew how proud Heath's words had made Jim feel.

'To Jim,' everyone called, downing their fizzy drinks and slapping him on the back before diving onto the table, emergency staff always ready to party.

'That was great, Heath.' Hannah's voice was choked as Heath came over. 'It will have meant a lot to Jim.'

'It's the truth,' Heath said easily. 'But, Hannah…' His voice lowered. 'There's no way there was enough in that envelope for that watch.'

'A couple of people put in after you.' Hannah blushed, shrinking under Heath's knowing gaze.

'Not that much, Hannah. How much extra did you end up putting in?'

'Just a few dollars. Please, don't make a big deal out of it, Heath,' Hannah begged as Jim started to make his way over. 'Jim's been really wonderful with all my problems with Ken. Don't say anything.'

'On one condition,' Heath warned. 'You catch up with me later and tell me what the difference was. OK?'

'OK!' Hannah snapped, then painted on a bright smile as the man of the moment joined them, proudly displaying his new watch for everyone to admire.

'I was hoping for a busy night,' Jim sighed. 'I'd like to go out with a bang.'

Hannah glanced down at his watch.

'There's still plenty of time for that yet, Jim.'

'Can you believe we've got a clear board?' Jayne smothered a yawn, staring around at the empty department. Every gurney had been stripped and remade, every trolley cleaned. The night seemed impossibly long with so few patients to fill it. Only Bella sat nervously bouncing her knee up and down, twisting a stray lock of hair round and round her finger, as the rest of the staff slumped lethargically. The students were on an extended meal break, and the other RNs were either taking the final patients up to the wards or around in the overnight obs ward, trying to calm an elderly Alzheimer's patient who had risen before the sun and was loudly demanding to go home this very instant!

'Who are those two guys in the waiting room? I might go and tell them to move.'

'They've got a niece or something on the children's ward.' Bella answered Jayne quickly, using the line that had been rehearsed in case anyone asked about the undercover detectives in the waiting room, especially conspicuous now that the department was empty. 'They didn't want to go home, but there's only one family member allowed to stay up on the ward, so I said it would be OK if they waited here.'

'Fair enough. Don't,' she groaned as Heath came over, yawning. 'It's infectious, you know.'

'I'm bored,' Heath whined like a petulant two-year-old.

'Then why don't you go and lie down in the on-call room?' Jayne suggested.

'Because the second I close my eyes, no doubt something will come in.'

'We won't call you unless it's serious,' Jayne responded, shooing him off. 'Go and put your head down for a couple of hours. If nothing comes in, I'll give you a knock before I go off duty.'

Heath didn't need to be asked a third time, taking off his white coat and stethoscope in record time and tossing them over a chair. 'You'll call me?' he checked, but didn't wait for an answer, heading straight for the on-call room, happy to grab a couple of hours' sleep whenever he could get it.

'I suppose I should try and get some rosters done,' Jayne sighed with a distinct lack of enthusiasm. 'Or I could just make another cup of coffee.'

'Coffee sounds good.' Hannah looked up from the magazine she was reading. 'Do you want me to make it?'

'I'll do it,' Jayne said, getting up.

Bella stood up as well. 'I'll go and check on the guys in the waiting room, see if they want me to ring up to the ward for them for any news.'

'It's like a bloody ghost town,' Detective Miller moaned as soon as Bella came over.

'Tell me about it. The only controlled drug that's been given is 50 milligrams of pethidine, and everything seemed in order. Except for one thing,' Bella added, almost as an afterthought, not sure whether or not it was relevant. 'Hannah told me she gave Jayne a leaving present to lock up in the drug cupboard.'

'Has it gone missing?'

'Nothing like that.' Bella shook her head. 'It's just that when Jayne and I checked the pethidine, Jayne seemed surprised to see it there, as if Hannah hadn't told her. It could be nothing, it could have just slipped her mind, I guess.'

'Look, you'd better get back to it,' Detective Miller said. 'Just keep your eyes and ears open. There's something going on.'

'There's nothing going on,' Bella insisted. 'We couldn't have picked a more ordinary night. There's nothing going to go down.'

But Detective Miller shook his head. 'I can smell it, Bella, so keep your wits about you, because this is exactly the time when crimes happen—when you're least expecting it.'

The waiting-room door slid open then and Bella watched as Jim wheeled in a patient, assessing the situation in a matter of seconds.

In obvious pain, the man was clutching at his chest, and even though the few words he spoke weren't in English, Bella didn't need a translator to work out that he was in serious discomfort. She took the man's pulse as Jim deftly wheeled him straight through to Resus. Hannah put down her magazine and made her way over as Jim told them the little he knew.

'His family are just moving the car. None of them speak very good English but I think his name's Mr Kapur.'

'Thanks, Jim.' Hannah nodded gratefully, deftly applying a chest monitor as Bella did a swift set of obs, speaking all the while in reassuring tones, even though the patient probably didn't understand her, but even more so in this case a calm, assured demeanour was called for. 'Can you get IV access?' Hannah asked, programming the monitor to do a 12-lead ECG, which would give a comprehensive indication of the patient's cardiac status. 'And then we'd better give Heath a call.'

Just as Bella swabbed the area, needle poised at the back of a rather poor-looking vein, the emergency phone trilled loudly, and Bella looked up anxiously, before concentrating on the important task in hand.

'It's OK.' Hannah was looking over towards the nurses' station. 'Jayne's back. She's picking up the phone.

'Well done,' she added as the cannula slipped into place on Bella's first attempt, handing over some tape so that she could secure the access.

'Jim's big bang's about to come off.' Jayne made her way over swiftly to deliver the news. 'We've got a single vehicle motor accident. Three passengers, two adults and one child. Multiple injuries is all the information we've got at this stage. I'll start setting up and call down the trauma team. Hannah, buzz round to the girls in the obs ward and tell one of them to come back. Jess should be back from the ward at any moment, she'll run anyway when she hears the overhead chimes. Bella, can you go and wake up Heath?'

Running through the department, her rubber soles barely making a sound, Bella almost skidded into Jim, who was guiding Mr Kapur's relatives through to the interview room.

'There's a multi-trauma coming in,' Bella called out to him, and Jim gave a knowing nod, heading straight off towards Resus to see what Jayne wanted him to do.

Knocking loudly on Heath's door, Bella suppressed a smile as she heard a sleepy curse. The door opened a matter of seconds later, his usually immaculate hair sticking up at right angles, the crease marks from a pillow on the side of his face. Never had he looked more gorgeous.

'Multiple trauma coming in.' Bella explained as Heath pulled on his shoes and followed her out, raking fingers through his hair as he walked. Almost annoyingly, Bella noted, his hair fell into perfect shape. 'Two adults and a child. That's all we've got so far.'

'OK, call down the trauma team.'

'Done,' Bella responded. 'There's a chest pain just come in as well, although he doesn't looked too bad at this stage. We've got IV access.'

They were at Resus now. Nurses were gathering around the beds as the trauma team started to arrive. Not a single yawn came from anyone, adrenaline already starting to kick in as they awaited the arrival of the patients. Immediately Heath made his way over to Mr Kapur, introducing himself to the bewildered man and then listening carefully to his chest with his stethoscope before reading the ECG.

'Does any of his family speak English?' he asked after a few fruitless attempts at trying to get a history from Mr Kapur.

'None of them, I'm afraid,' Hannah answered. 'I've just been out to the waiting room to try and get a better history but I couldn't get them to understand. They gave me some Anganine tablets that have his name on them, so I guess we at least know he suffers from angina.'

'I think it's angina he's got now,' Heath said, 'but we'd better take some blood and check his troponin levels just in case he is having an infarct. I'll get Cardiology to come straight down and assess him. If these three are badly injured, we're going to be busy.

'This is your fault, Jayne.' Heath gave a slow lazy smile, assuming control and calming everyone at the same time. 'I told you I shouldn't have gone to bed.'

As the blue lights flashed past the window, all joking was put on hold, all faces grim as they awaited their patients, everyone in the room aware that this was probably a family that might just have been torn apart.

'Driver!' a breathless paramedic announced, following Heath's command and taking him to the far end bed. 'He was unconscious on arrival, his GCS was only five at the scene, but he's picked up since then and it's lifted to ten. He's really irritable.' The rapid shorthand that was delivered as the patient was carefully lifted over to the waiting bed told the gathered staff a lot. The normal GCS score was fifteen, and the man lying on the bed was a dangerous way off that figure. Clearly disorientated, he was moaning and thrashing around the bed, one hand twitching ominously, Bella had the uneasy feeling he was about to start to convulse.

'Have we got a name?' the anaesthetist called, flashing a light into the man's pupils and doing a rapid assessment, then calling for anticonvulsants as the patient went into a full-blown convulsion.

'Patrick O'Keefe, according to his driver's licence,' the paramedic answered, watching as the patient's fit was swiftly brought under control and the anaesthetist made the decision to paralyse and intubate him, inserting a tube down his throat to take over the patient's breathing while they concentrated on his injuries. 'Though it's an overseas one. Apparently they were on their way to the airport. Some end to their holiday. Some families have all the bad luck...'

Horrified, Bella watched as Heath closed his eyes in a tiny moment of regret, his grim face tensing further as the resus doors slid open again and their worst fears were confirmed. The pale, terrified features of Lucy came into sharp focus, her glorious headscarf wrapped around her neck, her tiny frame racked with frightened sobs as the paramedics wheeled her in.

'Take her, Bella,' Heath ordered, his voice unusually tense as he headed over to Patrick. 'She needs a familiar face.'

Hands shaking involuntarily, Bella listened to the paramedic's handover as she gently slipped Lucy into a hospital gown, retrieving the scarf and tying it around her smooth, bald head before recording a set of obs. She desperately tried to console her terrified patient, but knew how hollow her comforting words sounded to a woman who had already been through way too much and had to face yet more.

'My daughter, Marnie.' Lucy was inconsolable, saying her child's name over and over. 'She was screaming. Where is she?'

'She's coming in,' Bella said gently. 'The paramedics said she was in the ambulance behind.'

'She was screaming so loudly. The poor child was terrified.'

'That's good,' Bella soothed. 'I know that sounds like a strange thing to say, but the fact she was screaming is actually a good sign, Lucy. It means that she's conscious.'

While the conversation was going on Bella was observing her patient, doing a set of obs and then assisting Heath in his examination when he finally came over, leaning Lucy forward as Heath listened to her frail chest, then laying her down as he gently probed her flat stomach. There was not a pound of spare flesh on Lucy's tiny emaciated body, and not for the first time Bella wondered just how much one person was supposed to take.

'You've got some bruising across your chest,' Heath explained gently, 'which normally wouldn't be serious, but we're going to need to admit you, Lucy. We need to check your bleeding times…'

'Don't worry about me. What about Marnie? What about Patrick?'

'Patrick's been sedated.' Heath spoke very slowly and clearly. 'When he first came in to us he started to convulse so the anaesthetist has put a tube down to help with his breathing, just until we know what's going on and he's a bit more stable. The neurosurgeon has come down and Patrick's going straight round for a CAT scan. As soon as we've got the results we'll know more.'

Lucy was consoled only for a second as piercing screams filled the air, Lucy sat bolt upright, 'That's Marnie,' she wailed, and if she'd had an ounce of strength left in her, Bella would have sworn Lucy would have climbed down from the trolley there and then.

'Heath's with her,' Bella said consolingly, saying it over and over, trying to somehow get through. She was tempted to go and have a look for herself how the little girl was but decided it was better to stay put, knowing Lucy needed someone with her during this harrowing time.

'She needs me,' Lucy sobbed. 'And I'm not there for her. I'm never going to be able to be there for her!'

'You'll always be there for her,' Bella responded, her nose starting to run, tears springing in her own eyes as she held this precious lady, understanding the bigger picture without further need for explanation. 'You're always going to be her mum no matter what happens.'

'Lucy.' Heath's face was serious as he came over, but he managed a tiny positive smile, enough to instantly reassure the anxious woman a touch. 'Marnie's OK. She's fractured her left femur, but apart from that she's going OK. We're just putting some traction on her leg, which will make her a lot more comfortable, and we're going to get her something now for pain. As soon as she's had that I'll wheel you in beside her.'

'Promise?'

'I promise.' Heath nodded, holding her eyes for a firm second before turning to

Bella. 'Everyone's tied up. Jayne's putting on the traction, Hannah's in CT with Patrick. Can you check some pethidine with me? And the cardiologist wants some morphine for Mr Kapur.'

'I don't like to leave her,' Bella mouthed, but Lucy was too sharp to miss a trick.

'I'm not going to do anything stupid. Just get my baby the medicine she needs.'

'I hate this job.' Whistling it through tense lips, finally Heath let his emotions slip as the drug room door closed firmly behind them. 'How bloody unfair is that?'

'Totally,' Bella answered, watching as he buried his face in his hand for a moment, trying to compose himself.

'She's just so damned nice.' Indulgent moment over, he walked to the drug cupboard Bella was opening, barely paying attention as she pulled out the books and set up the kidney dishes and syringes. 'Do you know if they've got medical insurance?'

'They're covered for accidents,' Bella replied, pulling open the box of pethidine and flashing it at Heath. 'It's Lucy's cancer treatments they couldn't get any cover for.'

'Then she's to be admitted to the overnight obs ward till I discharge her,' Heath responded immediately. 'Any treatment she needs, this department covers, and I'll have a word with Craig Jenkins as well.'

'For now, let's just get Marnie her medication,' Bella broke in. 'OK, pethidine 50 milligrams in five mils, so I'll pull up 2.5—agreed?'

'Agreed.' Heath nodded as Bella pulled up the drug, taping a label to the ampoule and placing the kidney dish on the drug sheet. 'Sign the book, Heath.'

'For God's sake,' Heath said, urging her to hurry. 'We need to get back out there.'

'Well, do it right and we soon will be,' Bella snapped. She understood his urgency but a drug mistake was the last thing anyone needed now. 'Right, what's the next one?'

'Morphine, 5 milligrams.' Heath pulled out a new box. 'Sealed,' he said tersely, adhering to protocol. He ripped through the label, pulled open the box and flashed the contents at Bella. 'Ten ampoules.' Glancing up as she wrote in the drug book, Bella froze for a second, her face paling as she stared at the contents.

'This is saline, Heath!'

'It's a sealed box.' Heath shook his head as if clearing it. 'Pharmacy must have made a mistake.'

'Pharmacy doesn't make that sort of mistake.' Her mind spun into overdrive, trying to work out what to do first—whether to alert the detectives in the waiting room or to play the innocent a moment longer—but Heath was already making his moves, pulling out every last box of morphine and ripping them open, cursing out loud as again and again the same ampoules stared back at him.

'I'm calling the police.'

'Maybe we should let the nursing coordinator know,' Bella suggested, playing for time, trying to somehow stall him, to prevent him from storming out into the department, because from the tension in his face, any second now he was likely to blow the whole thing out of the water.

'Forget the nursing coordinator! Hell!' He whistled. 'There's fifty ampoules of morphine missing.' He was making to go, wrenching open the door, and Bella knew, just knew he was going to blast into the department, pick up the telephone and let rip, his whole body literally shaking with appalled rage that one of his staff would stoop so low.

'Heath wait!' In an instinctive motion she slammed the door closed, saw his confusion as he swung around to face her. 'Don't do anything yet.'

'What?' Appalled, he stared down at her. 'What are you saying here, Bella? Why the hell would you ask me not to do anything?

Are you trying to tell me you're involved with this?'

'Sort of.' She had to tell him, Bella knew that. Shaking her hand off his arm as if she were contaminated, he made to go and Bella knew he was going to blow the whistle and more than likely ruin the whole investigation.

She had no choice but to tell him.

'Heath.' Fishing in her pocket, she pulled out her ID. 'I'm a police officer.' She watched as he took in the badge, read her details in stunned silence. His eyes when he looked up were even more confused. 'The department's being watched. The police are already here—we need to catch this thief red-handed.'

'This is all a set-up.' He gestured to the pile of boxes, clearly horrified. 'Are you telling me that you put saline in the drug cupboard?'

'No.' Bella shook her head. She didn't have time for this, didn't have time to explain, and yet she somehow had to if she wanted to keep him calm. 'It was morphine that was put in the boxes, Heath. Some time tonight someone's got into the cupboard and swapped things over. I wasn't expecting this at all.'

'But they're sealed boxes.'

'Please, Heath.' Bella swallowed hard. 'I need you to go in there and carry on as normal.'

'Normal!' Heath roared. 'And I suppose you want me to give the cardiac patient a shot of saline as well.'

'Of course not,' Bella hissed, putting her finger to her lips begging him quiet. 'Say what you did when you first opened them, say that Pharmacy has made a mistake. Heath, you have to trust me here.'

'Trust you!' The look he shot conveyed his contempt, lips curling with disgust as he stared down at her. 'Hell, Bella, I don't even know you!'

CHAPTER TEN

'WHERE on earth have you two been?' Jayne looked up sharply as they both walked in.

'Believe me, Jayne, you don't want to know,' Heath drawled, and apart from a face as white as chalk and a muscle galloping in his cheek, he could have been chatting about the weather. 'Pharmacy's messed up.'

'Pharmacy?' Jayne frowned.

'They've only filled five boxes of morphine with saline, as if we don't have enough to worry about with drugs down here.'

'Saline?' Jayne repeated.

'Saline.' Heath nodded. 'Which isn't going to help the cardiac patient. Can someone ring around the wards, get some down here stat?'

'No need.' The cardiologist looked up. 'He's responding now to the Anganine.'

'OK,' Heath said. 'Well, can we just check off this pethidine for Marnie? Then maybe you can give Pharmacy a call, please, Bella.' For all the world it looked as if he was staring at her, but his eyes were looking straight through her. 'Let them know their mistake. You might do it a touch more gently than me, and tell them, please, to get some stock down here as soon as possible.'

'Sure,' Bella mumbled, checking Marnie's identity as safely and as quickly as she could before fleeing Resus, picking up the telephone and punching in a mobile number. She registered every detail, her eyes scanning the department. Day staff were starting to drift around now, taking over from the night shift in Resus, Jayne delivering the handover as Hannah and Jim wheeled Patrick back from his CT scan. Everything seemed normal, right down to the receptionist's annoyed frown as a mobile trilled in Reception.

Mumbling her findings into the telephone, Bella willed herself calm as she relayed her orders to Detective Miller because, even though she was as junior as a nearly detective could be, Bella was the one on the floor, Bella was the one running the show right now.

'What did they say?' Jayne came over as Bella put down the phone.

'They're going to send someone down as soon as they can.'

'And so they should,' Jayne tutted. 'Look, I hate to do this, Bella, I know it's been a long night and no doubt you're aching to get off, but you're going to need to—'

'Fill in an incident report,' Bella sighed, forcing a smile. 'Can I get a coffee first?'

'Of course. Look, I'd stick around, but I don't really know what I can tell them. The drugs were sealed when I checked them last night.'

'It's their mistake.' Bella shrugged. 'I'll grab a coffee and get writing.'

'And tell Heath to do one, too. Mind you, from the look on his face, he won't need re-minding, he's furious.'

'Do you blame him? What if that patient had really needed the morphine?' Her voice trailed off and she gave another shrug. 'I'll just ring my mum, let her know I'm going to be late.'

''Night, then.' Jayne smiled even though it was morning, but it was what every night nurse said.

''Night, Jayne.'

'How's Patrick?' Bella asked as Hannah made her way over, attempting to seem normal even though her heart was flickering faster than Mr Kapur's.

'Good!' Hannah enthused. 'Well, maybe that's a slight exaggeration, but there's no bleeding or infarct evident. The neurosurgeon thinks he should do well. Poor family,' Hannah added, wringing her hands. 'Next time I'm feeling sorry for myself I'm going to remember what they're going through.' She gave a weary smile. 'Better get home to Ken. 'Night, Bella.'

''Night, Hannah.'

Watching as Hannah headed towards the changing room, stopping to speak to Jim, Bella took a deep breath and picked up the phone, punching in the mobile number she'd learnt off by heart. It was answered on first ring and Bella didn't even need to speak.

'We've got him,' Detective Miller said without introduction. 'Phil's checked his bag and he's clean, Bella, there's nothing on him. Where is she now?'

'In the changing room,' Bella answered, her voice monotone. 'I'm going in there. Can you wait outside? I just want five minutes with her.'

'I hope to God you're right about this, Bella.'

Walking past Hannah and Jim, Bella made her way to the changing room, pushing the door open with moist palms, scarcely able to comprehend the enormity of what was about to take place, still, at this late stage, processing the facts in her mind, convincing herself over and over as she stepped inside that she was surely right, that what she had known all along could only be confirmed now.

She hadn't banked on Heath being in there, hadn't banked on Heath slamming his way around the changing room, trying to find change for the coffee-machine, shooting her a baleful look as she stepped inside.

'Everything all right, Bella?' Jayne asked, pulling her jacket out of her locker and slamming it closed, frowning as Bella came over, clearly not in the sunniest of moods.

'Not really,' Bella answered, pulling out her ID badge and showing it to her stunned colleague. 'Jayne, at this point I should tell you that I'm a police officer and I've been observing the department over the last few days. Would you mind showing me what's inside your bag?'

'I don't know what you're talking about,' Jayne started, angrily shaking her head and starting to walk off, but Bella stood firm.

'There are two detectives outside the door, Jayne. If you don't want a scene in front of everyone, I suggest you do as I say.'

'Please, Bella,' Jayne started, her face paling, tears welling in her eyes. 'It's not what you think. This isn't for me.'

'For Tony, then?' Bella sneered, and Jayne nodded. Burying her face in her hand, she sank down on the bench, but Bella stood unmoved, her eyes flicking to Heath who stood in stunned, appalled silence as his colleague admitted her guilt.

'Tony made me do it,' Jayne said imploringly. 'My son Shane's an addict. I just thought if I could get it for him, give him a reducing dose, then at least I'd know it was clean. It was only meant to be for him.'

'Till his so-called friends found out?' Detective Miller walked in then but no one looked up. Jayne stared at the floor, tears streaming down her cheeks as the world finally caught up, as Detective Miller opened up the zipper on her bag and flashed the contents for Bella to see.

'I didn't want to keep taking it. It was only supposed to be for Shane! I've never hurt anyone.'

'Read her her rights,' Detective Miller said, but Bella shook her head. There was no thrill to be had here, just a nauseating taste at the back of her throat.

'Would you?'

It was horrible to see a dignified, educated woman reduced to this, to watch as she was read her rights and handcuffed and led outside through the department she'd served, to nod as Detective Miller told Bella he'd meet her back at the station when she'd collected up her stuff.

'Enjoy that, did you?' Heath's voice was flat as he stared coolly at Bella. 'Is that how you get your kicks?'

'No one enjoys this,' Bella attempted, but Hugh flicked her response away.

'Rubbish. You'll be down the pub celebrating your little win tonight, Bella. You know it as well as I do. Were the handcuffs really necessary, Bella? Did you have to rub her face in it a bit further? You heard what

Jayne said. She was trying to support her son's habit, trying to get him off drugs.'

'And failing,' Bella pointed out. 'And getting herself in a whole lot deeper than she ever imagined. She's recruiting domestic staff to help her, Heath. Tony has been helping her. No doubt he locked himself in his cleaning cupboard tonight after Jayne got the drugs, filling the packets up with saline and resealing them so that Jayne could put them back.'

'How do you know all this?' Heath asked, clearly bewildered. 'How did you know it was Jayne?'

'I guessed on my first day. You were right—she did overreact about that ampoule of morphine that hadn't been signed for, and with good reason. Drugs going missing while she'd been on holiday would undoubtedly take the heat off, and the way she consistently defended Tony even when it was clear he wasn't doing his job just didn't make any sense.'

'She was only trying to help her son!' Heath roared.

'This wasn't a couple of paracetemol she was taking here, Heath. She's been stealing drugs and handing them over to Tony to deal with. Slipping boxes under the drug book after two staff members have signed. And if you're going to say that no one got hurt, then you're wrong. Do you remember Benjamin Evans, that man who fell off his ladder and lay in this department, sobbing with back pain? Well, the second urine specimen I took from him confirmed that he didn't have any drugs in his system. Jayne clearly decided he didn't need it as badly as she did.'

'No.' Heath shook his head, despite the irrefutable evidence, loyal to his staff to the end. 'She'd never do that. Jayne's a good nurse.'

'*Was* a good nurse, Heath,' Bella corrected him. 'Mr Evans lay in agony for two hours when it could have been avoided, and I've got Mr Evans's urinalysis result back at the

station if you don't believe me. I've got cop-
ies of all the pager traces, too. Jayne paged
herself that morning, knowing full well that
she'd be disturbed and she'd have an excuse
to be called away and swap the syringe.
Suppose Mr Kapur had needed that morphine, Heath? Suppose Lucy O'Keefe had
been in terminal pain?'

'Am I supposed to clap?' Heath sneered.
'Supposed to offer my congratulations?'

'I'm just trying to make you understand
the gravity of what Jayne was doing.'

'And what about you?' Heath's eyes were
like ice as he stared back at her, his stance
utterly immovable as he hurled hurtful words
across the room. 'You used me, Bella,
screwed me in the hope of getting inside information on Jayne.'

'It wasn't like that,' Bella started, then
closed her mouth in defeat as reality dawned
for Heath.

'So I was a suspect, too?' He let out an
incredulous, mirthless laugh. 'Were you go-

ing through my drawers and cupboards after I'd left, checking for track marks when you undressed me?'

'No.' Bella shook her head in desperate denial. 'It wasn't anything like that.' But Heath was on a roll now, hurling insult after insult, clearly incensed and refusing to listen to reason. 'Lying through your teeth so that I'd open up to you. All that guff about Danny, all that—'

'Everything I said about Danny was true,' Bella pleaded, willing him to try and at least understand. 'And I didn't screw you, Heath, we made love.'

'Oh, you screwed me,' Heath shouted. 'Every which way you could.'

'I couldn't tell you what I was doing, Heath, surely you can see that, but every other thing I said was true.'

'Save it, Bella.'

'What happened to that big speech about acceptance, Heath? This is my job, this is what I do, and I'm not ashamed of it. Jayne deserves everything she gets as far as I'm concerned. She's let everyone down, including her profession. Yes, maybe I will have that drink tonight after all. Maybe I will toast a job well done.'

'Bella…' Hannah nervously peered around the door, her eyes red from crying, and Bella regretted her words immediately.

'I'm sorry.' Bella swallowed. 'You didn't deserve to hear that.'

'I agree with you,' Hannah said surprisingly. 'I'm devastated, of course, but I know you're right. I trusted Jayne completely. I'd have trusted her with my kids, my husband. You're right, she's let us all down. But this isn't about Jayne, Bella.' Coming over, Hannah looked her in the eye and Bella felt her heart still as Hannah gave her that sympathetic, hesitant look Bella had used so many times herself when she was about to deliver bad news.

'We've just had an alert from Ambulance Control. They're bringing in a young man from a nursing home for palliative care, but apparently he's taken a turn for the worse in the ambulance. His name's Danny Burgess. His parents just called through from their car phone…' The world seemed to stop. She could see Hannah's mouth moving, even hear what she was saying, but her mind literally froze as she tried to take in what she was being told. 'They're on their way, but they said he was your fiancé, that maybe you were here and could be with him for them.'

'For them?' Anguished eyes lifted, horrible truth dawning as Hannah gently took her arm and sat her on the bench.

'Danny might not make it till they get here.'

The words thudded in one by one, each one imploding on the other till all she could hear was her pulse pounding in her temples. Acrid bile rose in her throat and Bella truly thought she was about to faint, but Hannah was holding her arms, holding her steady as she digested the news. 'Is he in pain?' Her voice sounded normal but her body was trembling. A million questions raced through her mind, but she was only able to voice one right now.

'Not according to Ambulance Control,' Hannah said softly as Bella sniffed loudly, trying to compose herself, trying to be brave for the worst moment of her life. Looking up, she halted Heath, who was coming over towards her, with a look, stopping him in his tracks, her eyes warning him to stay out of it.

'Thank God,' Bella replied, leaning on Hannah's arm and walking shakily towards the door. 'You wouldn't want to be dying in agony in this place.'

CHAPTER ELEVEN

'OH, DANNY.'

Climbing into the ambulance, Bella took his hand, not caring if she was in the way as the paramedics prepared to unload him, not even listening as they gave Heath the hand-over, just vaguely aware of Hannah's hand on her shoulder as Danny was wheeled inside. She made a mental note to thank Hannah for staying back, for holding her up when she thought she might fall. Seeing him lying there so tall and gorgeous and somehow, despite it all, still proud, nothing else mattered any more. Jayne, Heath, Detective Miller all flew out of her mind. She just focused on the one person who really mattered now, the one person who deserved her undivided attention—for a little while longer at least.

'Why aren't we going to Resus?' As they glided into a cubicle and the paramedics started to lift him over to the gurney, Bella could hear the hysterical note in her rising voice amid the calm order of the room.

'He's not for active treatment, Bella,' Heath said, gently pulling her outside as Hannah assisted the paramedics. 'We're just to make him comfortable.'

'No!' Furious in denial, she shook her head. 'Then why is he here? If he's just to be made comfortable, why the hell did the nursing home call an ambulance and drag him out of bed?'

'He needed suctioning,' Heath broke in gently, 'He needed full nursing care to make him comfortable, and the home don't have the staff to provide it.'

It didn't make sense, none of it made sense. The last time she'd seen Danny he'd been sitting up, off his food perhaps, but sitting up none the less. But now...

'He developed a chest infection last night,' Heath explained, and she closed her eyes in regret, rueing the fact she hadn't been home, riddled with guilt that the one time he'd needed her, the one time she'd let down her guard and started to live, Danny had started to die. And she hadn't been there for him, hadn't been in his corner, fighting, as horrible decisions had been made. Bella took Danny's warm hand, holding it in hers, watching the rapid rise and fall of his chest, taking in the flushed face and parched lips. 'The nursing home's GP came out and started him on antibiotics, but the infection was overwhelming and he developed sepsis. He hasn't responded to the antibiotics.'

'But there are different antibiotics...' Bella said, tears coming thick and fast now, desperate to be back in there beside him, yet knowing if she did she'd be letting him go, that it would all be over. 'He needs to be in Resus. You need to do something, Heath.

He's not even thirty years old, for God's sake!'

'According to Danny's notes and the letter from the nursing home, his parents agreed last night that he wasn't for aggressive treatment, that in the event of a cardiac arrest he wasn't to be resuscitated.'

'No.' Bella shook her head, simply refusing to accept it.

'Joyce and Joe would never have agreed to that!' Perplexed, Bella shook her head. 'Never,' she insisted, panic welling inside her, sure that somewhere along the line someone had got things wrong. 'They still think he's going to get better one day.' She was shouting now, and it felt like before, felt like she was back to where it had all started, screaming for the staff to listen, to understand that Danny was really ill. 'They think that we'll get married one day—'

'No, Bella, we don't.'

Joyce Burgess's voice was firm as she made her way over, looking so much older than her fifty-five years, way too much pain etched on her face, the small ray of hope that had kept her going through this never-ending nightmare extinguished now, and it showed. Every line on her face deeper, tired eyes swollen from crying and yet there was an air of quiet dignity about her that reminded Bella of Danny as Joyce took her hand. 'He's had enough, Bella.'

And she knew then it must be true. Joyce was giving in, Joyce the mother who had fought tooth and nail, had guarded her son so fiercely through these terrible times. She would never let go unless it really was over.

'I need to be with him, Bella, and so do you.'

And she did.

But first there was something she needed to do. As Danny's parents made their way into the cubicle Bella hesitated outside and looked up at Heath. Seeing the compassion overriding the anger in his expression, she screwed her eyes closed for a moment, leaving it to Heath to fill the horrible silence.

'You have nothing to feel guilty—'

'Don't!' Holding up a trembling hand, she halted him. 'Please, don't, Heath. I need to ask you something. If it doesn't cause you any problems, would you mind...?' Her voice petered out, but Heath finished her sentence for her.

'You want me to hand Danny's care over?'

Bella nodded. 'Please.'

'I'll let Martin Elmes know now.'

'It's nothing to do with your medical skills—'

'Bella,' Heath broke in. 'You don't need to explain, I understand.'

She was grateful for that at least. Grateful to Heath for keeping his distance. Danny deserved her undivided attention, deserved her absolute love for a little while longer, and deserved that last piece of dignity. Because, Bella realized as she walked inside and joined his parents, if it had been her lying there, if it had been the other way around, as much as she'd perhaps have understood, as much as she'd maybe have wanted Danny to move on, she wouldn't have wanted his new lover looking after her.

He deserved so much more.

As Joyce held Danny's hand, Bella brushed back his damp hair, tracing his eyebrows with her fingers, whispering gentle words of love as she did so.

'Can I do anything for you?' Hannah asked, her presence comforting but not intrusive, a privileged spectator, just there to support, no offence taken when no one looked up or answered.

'I'm just going to give Danny a small injection.' Moving the blanket slightly, Hannah went on, her voice low and reassuring. 'It's called atropine. It will dry up some of the secretions and make Danny's breathing a bit more comfortable.' Swabbing his leg, Hannah replaced the blanket. 'Now, would you like me to take out his NG tube?' Still with her eyes on Danny, Bella gave a small nod.

'Please. He always hated it.' As Hannah went to put on gloves, Bella changed her mind, gently removing the tape from around his nose and performing the small task herself, wanting to do this for him, wanting to do something, *anything* to make this a little bit better for Danny. Gently taking out the wretched NG tube he hated so much, Bella held his hand and kissed his cheek over and over as his breathing slowed down, aware only peripherally of Joyce and Joe, and Hannah a solid support to all. Just taking every step of his final journey as far as she could with him, loving Danny as he deserved to be loved, wishing it could all somehow have been different, wishing quite simply that it didn't have to be so.

'It isn't fair,' Joe said when finally it was over, finally breaking down as he said goodbye to four years of hope.

'No,' Bella whispered, eyes curiously dry, numb with shock and exhaustion. 'None of this is fair.'

There it was.

The sky just as blue as ever, tiny cotton-wool wisps of cloud burning away as the day warmed up, the air a touch stale outside Emergency, bins overflowing with cigarette butts and coffee cups, taxis pulling up at the rank and ambulances lined up waiting for their next call.

Just the same as the last time she'd been there, only this time Danny was missing, missing from a world he had loved so much.

'Can I give you a lift, honey?'

Tired, tense, lighting a cigarette even as the sliding doors closed behind her, Hannah was there, just as she'd always been since Bella's first day. Shooting a wink to an in-secure newbie, holding the fort when the big guns had gone home and staying way over when she'd really been needed.

'No, thanks.' Bella gave a pale smile. 'I'm just catching my breath for a few moments, then I'd better head down to the station.'

'Shouldn't you be going home?'

'Probably,' Bella admitted. 'I'll just pop my head in, make sure they've got all the information they need from me.'

'About Jayne…' Hannah said, and her voice was so gentle, so kind, so worried Bella felt as if she might dissolve there and then.

'I'm sorry.' Her words strangled in her throat. 'I know you probably all hate me. I know you think—'

'No.' Hannah shook her head. 'No, you don't know what I think, Bella. Every time I come on shift I try to treat people the same way I'd want my own family to be treated. Try to smile when it's horrible. My poor Ken's got MS. He's forty-five going on a hundred, and a more miserable, selfish man you couldn't meet. Do this, get that, lift my leg, no, not that one. How I haven't strangled him with my own bare hands I wonder myself sometimes. But I love him, Bella. I know that it's all a show, know that it's his way of staying in control when he's lost everything else. Sometimes we end up here, more often than not at three in the morning, because his catheter's blocked or his temperature's high, and every time I hold my breath, every time I wait for someone to snap, to moan when he rings the bell for the fiftieth time or tells the doctor he's way too young to know what he's doing...'

She was trying to be nice, trying and somehow failing to say the right thing and Bella couldn't deal with it now. She screwed her eyes closed, willing Hannah to be quiet, to just go for a while and leave her alone.

'I trust those guys and girls, trust them to know that as bad as it is for them to have Ken on their shift, I've got him day in day out at home. And do you know what, Bella? Not once to date have they let me down. Till today.'

Tired eyes met Bella's.

'Jayne, for whatever reasons, was following a different agenda. You can't do that in nursing.'

'When I took this job,' Bella gulped, 'I told them that I wouldn't compromise patient care, that whatever the cost to the case, while I was there—'

'Because you're a nurse,' Hannah broke in. 'Because that's what you are. There's a little piece inside you that a copper's uniform will never take away...' Her voice trailed off as she looked over Bella's shoulder. She patted Bella on the arm and Bella knew, without looking, why. Knew without turning her head that Heath was beside her.

'She's talking about driving herself down to the station, Heath,' Hannah said in a dry voice. 'Can you talk some sense into her?'

'Leave it to me.' Heath smiled, but it was guarded. He nodded as Hannah drifted away, his hand reaching out for Bella then retracting as Bella pulled away, staring into the murky depths of her cold hot chocolate and trying to think of something to say but coming up with nothing.

'You can't drive,' Heath said eventually. 'Let me at least see you home.'

'I need to go to the station first.' She saw the doubt cloud his eyes, but Bella stood firm. 'I really do need to.'

'Then let me take you.'

Too tired to argue, too wrapped up in her own emotions to even contemplate his, she let him lead her, stood as he opened the passenger door of the car, as docile as a sleepy child, sat as he clipped her in, tears filling her eyes and drying, a scream building in her throat then dissolving as she stared at the brown walls of Emergency, scarcely able to comprehend that Danny was in there, that, for him, it really was all over.

She didn't notice that they drove in silence. Only when Heath pulled up at the police station did Bella even realize they were there.

'I'll wait for you...' Heath offered, but Bella shook her head.

'Please, don't. I've no idea how long I'll be.'

'It doesn't matter how long you are, I'm happy to—'

'One of my colleagues will give me a lift home,' Bella broke in and pulled open the passenger door, knowing he would call her back but beating him to it.

'I know you hate me for lying, Heath, I know that perhaps it was wrong, but I'm not going to apologize for what I did.' She watched as his fingers tightened around the steering-wheel, his jaw quilting as he clearly held back from saying what was on his mind.

'Hannah gave Danny an injection before...' She saw a tiny frown flicker between his eyes, knew he had no idea where this was leading. 'And I knew, without thought or hesitation, that Hannah was acting in Danny's interest. I don't need to tell you what Danny, his parents and myself have been through. Today was the end of an agonizing journey and how it played out was entrusted to people like Hannah and yourself to make it not any better but certainly not any worse for us. Patients and their families don't question what we're doing to them. Oh, they might ask what a drug is called, or what it's for, but they never question that we have anything other than their best interests at heart. That's just as it should be, a natural assumption. Jayne's maybe taken that away from your department. If this gets into the papers...' She took a deep breath. 'It was Jayne who let you down, Heath. Not me.'

'You let me down, Bella.' She could hear the strangled emotion in his voice. 'We made love, you let me love a person I thought I knew.'

'That *was* me.' Anguished eyes turned to him. 'And as much as I wanted to tell you, I couldn't.' She saw him shake his head, saw him open his mouth to argue, and her voice grew more insistent. 'I couldn't, Heath,' she reiterated. 'Sleeping with you had nothing to do with the case. In fact, it was possibly the most stupid thing I could have done, but it happened in spite of my work, in spite of everything that was happening in my life. My fiancé was dying and we were making love, you were a suspect in a case I was investigating. There were plenty of reasons not to get close to you, but it happened in spite of everything.'

'Did you ever think it was me?' It was as if he couldn't even bear to look at her any more, staring fixedly ahead as he spoke.

'No.' Her voice was tiny. 'Heath, I knew almost from the start that it was Jayne.'

'Suppose you'd been wrong? Suppose you'd found out that I was involved. What would you have done?'

'Exactly what I did to Jayne.'

Finally he looked at her, but it was like looking at a stranger. Hurt, pain, and anger were etched on every feature.

'Just suppose that I had told you the truth, Heath. You've worked with Jayne for years. Can you honestly say you wouldn't have warned her, tried to talk some sense into her before it was too late?'

'What do you take me for?' Heath argued.

'A friend, a colleague, a leader of a close-knit team,' Bella said softly. 'You've known Jayne for years, you wouldn't be human if you didn't want to try and help her. I couldn't risk it, Heath. You have to understand that. I'm trying to become a detective and that will mean there's always going to be a part of me I can't reveal, there's always going to be things I cannot discuss.' She watched his eyes shutter, watched him slowly, wearily shake his head.

And maybe it was too much of an ask from a guy who had been let down before, and maybe today just wasn't the day to be moving on. She stepped out of the car, stared at the firm set of his profile and knew he was as raw and as immovable as her.

'Go home, Heath,' she said softly, closing the door behind her. 'Please.'

CHAPTER TWELVE

'THANKS for coming in.' Detective Miller wrapped a big arm around Bella's shoulders and gave her a comforting squeeze, and the sudden tender side of the man, brought fresh tears to her eyes. Her colleagues were the toughest of the lot and yet they supported each other, no questions asked, and could always be depended on to pull together in tough times. 'The hospital called and told us what happened with Danny. How are you coping?'

'I'm not sure yet,' Bella sniffed. 'Look, I'm sorry, Detective Miller, but I don't think I can face Jayne. I'm not sure I could hold it together long enough to interview her.'

'That's my department anyway.' Detective Miller smiled. 'You're not a detective, remember?'

Bella wearily nodded.

'Yet.'

Blinking up at him, she saw that he was smiling.

'I've already written my letter of recommendation. You've been great, Bella, and we're all agreed, and we can't wait to have you on board.'

Strange that in a day when she'd lost so much, one of her dreams should come true, that even in darkest time a tiny glimmer of a silver lining could frame the darkest cloud. And some way, somehow Bella knew that Danny had a hand in this, that this was Danny's way of allowing her to move on. And it was that knowledge that kept the tears back, allowed her to shake Detective Miller's hand and thank him for the opportunity.

'You had Jayne picked out from day one, didn't you?' Detective Miller led her through the maze of corridors through to the interview rooms, talking as he went. 'Personally I had my money on Hannah.'

'Hannah wouldn't harm a fly.' Bella smiled. 'Mind you, I admit even I started to have my doubts when I saw that watch in the cupboard and Jayne said she didn't know how it had got there.'

'She was planting a seed,' Detective Miller said wisely. 'Covering her tracks just in case she got caught. I have no doubt she'd have turned it on Hannah to save herself. Jayne was just letting you think that Hannah had been in the drug cupboard unescorted, in case she needed that later.'

'She was really that devious?'

'She was desperate,' Detective Miller said. 'You really never thought it was Hannah, even for a moment? Even when she practically admitted that her husband smoked pot?'

'No.' Bella shook her head. 'You're not going to do anything about that, are you?'

'About what?' Detective Miller winked, letting Bella know it was already forgotten.

'When she said about that drug being more than enough to pay for her new car battery,

I knew there and then for sure that she was innocent. That's the kind of throw-away comment people make when they've got nothing to hide.'

'What about Heath?' Detective Miller paused at a door, watched as a blush darkened her pale cheeks. 'What would you have done if he had been involved?'

'He asked me the same thing.' Tired, red-rimmed eyes stared back at her superior. 'And I'll tell you what I told him—had I been wrong, had Heath been involved, then I'd have done exactly the same with him as I did with Jayne.'

'Remember that feeling,' Detective Miller answered with more than a trace of urgency. 'Hold on to that voice inside you that tells you what's wrong and what's right, because it's easy to lose it sometimes.' Pushing open the door, he led her into a room and Bella made her way over to the two-way mirror, closing her eyes in regret for a moment as she saw Jayne alone and frail, sitting at a table in the interview room on the other side of the mirror, her head in her hands, shoulders heaving as she wept, a more lonely sight than Bella had ever seen.

'I feel sorry for her,' Bella said slowly, almost wishing she could walk next door, talk to Jayne as a friend instead of an officer.

'So do I.' Detective Miller's admission caught her unawares and she turned in surprise, looking up at the hardened but somehow kind face. 'I spoke to her for an hour before you arrived and she sang like a lark, didn't even want to wait for a solicitor. If anything, she's relieved that it's all finally out in the open. Her son has a drug problem and Jayne was terrified of him using dirty needles or getting contaminated drugs, so she started stealing in the hope she could wean him off herself. And, as you know, then his friends found out. Jayne wasn't recruiting domestic staff to help her...' He paused as Bella frowned.

'But I'm sure Tony was involved...'

'Oh, he's involved all right,' Detective Miller agreed. 'But Jayne didn't engineer the role for him, he took that on himself. He's been intimidating Jayne at every turn, watching her every move, threatening her when she got home. Every time he got told off for the floor not being clean or tissues not being replaced, Jayne took the brunt of it when she got home. Her intentions may have started off good, but she ended up mixing with a very nasty crowd. She found herself in way over her head and couldn't see a way out.'

'What will happen to her?' Bella asked.

'Well, she's co-operating and hopefully with a good solicitor she might even get a suspended sentence, given that it's a first offence. She'll never hold drug keys again, though.'

'Which is just as well,' Bella sighed. 'I suppose she could go into the rehab field, put some of those good intentions to proper use.'

'It's not our problem, though, Bella. What Jayne does with her life from this point is up to her. As for that Tony—' Detective Miller's face was grim '—he's a nasty piece. He's covered his tracks very well and we're going to have one hell of a job building a decent case against him. That's why I need you here today. I need to run everything by you before I go in and interview him. We need something to pin on him and so far all we've got is Jayne's evidence, which is hardly going to stand up in court as reliable.'

'I've told you everything I know.' Bella raked a hand through her hair, chewing on her lip, going over and over the thought process that had led her towards Tony. 'He was so surly, so lazy and Jayne consistently covered for him.'

'That's not enough.' Detective Miller shook his head. 'There's nothing on the tapes. Jayne was giving him the drugs, I'm sure of that, and he was depositing them into her bag at the nurses' station when he emptied the bin, but there's nothing to prove that. There are no cameras in domestics' cleaning cupboards, and he knew that. Jayne gave him that morphine last night and he replaced it with saline, but how do we prove it? He's sitting in the interview room laughing in our faces, more than happy to let Jayne carry the can.'

'There are cameras in Pharmacy, though.' Despite the utter wretchedness of the day, a glimmer of excitement welled inside her, the unbeatable thrill of solving a puzzle, the Rubik's Cube slotting into place with one final twist. But Detective Miller shook his head.

'He didn't take any drugs from Pharmacy. Everything's double-locked…'

'Except the stickers,' Bella said triumphantly. 'Tony cleans the floors in Pharmacy. There's a table in the middle where they check drugs, and there are the ''sealed and checked'' labels. I'll guarantee that he took a box, knowing it would come in useful later.'

'And it did.'

Bella gave an excited nod. 'After Jayne had given him the boxes, I bet he took them into the cleaning room and replaced the contents before resealing them. Go over the tapes, Detective Miller. You might not catch him actually doing it, but I can guarantee that there will be a box of stickers suddenly missing from the desk while he's mopping.'

'Got him.' Detective Miller grinned.

'Got him.' Bella almost smiled but it changed midway. Now she could finally let go, now her work was finished. The day was catching up with her and Detective Miller noticed.

'I'll get someone to drive you home.'

He walked her to the front of the building, having a brief word on the way with a colleague, Andy, who took Bella's arm and led her to a patrol car outside.

And for a tiny, stupid second Bella looked around, blinking in the bright sunlight, her eyes raking the street for a glimpse of a silver car with a blond unshaven guy dozing in the driver's seat, berating herself for even hoping that Heath might have ignored her plea.

For even daring to dream, after all that had taken place, that Heath might still be waiting for her.

CHAPTER THIRTEEN

RELIEF.

Hugging Danny's parents goodbye, the sermon still ringing in her ears, never had Bella felt more guilty for the emotion that washed over her: relief that finally this torture was over, that finally she could move on with her life.

'Stay for another drink,' Joyce offered. 'At least have something more to eat.'

'I have to go, Joyce.' Bella's voice was gentle but firm. 'I'm supposed to be back at work tomorrow and my car's still at the hospital. There's a million things I have to do.'

And there were.

Hollow with grief, the last few days had passed by in a blur. Family coming over at all hours, Joyce constantly on the telephone, planning a funeral that had taken place four years ago in Bella's mind yet going through the motions.

Dressing for Danny, just one more time. Tying her hair up neatly then taking it down, remembering how he'd liked it loose, adding just a touch of blusher to her cheeks and pouring on the final dregs of a bottle of perfume he'd given her on their last real Christmas together.

And despite all the support, despite family and friends doing their utmost to help, the utmost to make things easier for Bella, it had barely touched her.

The one person she'd needed for support during this black period in her life had been conspicuous by his absence. Oh, she'd never have taken him to the funeral. Bella had more tact than that. But to know in her own mind that Heath was beside her would have helped in so many more ways than one.

Tomorrow she would step back on the merry-go-round again. Climb back onto a world that had paused in Bella's mind for a few days but had carried on turning, no matter what was going on. Her compassionate leave had already run out.

Five days was apparently more than enough to get over a man who should have been her fiancé. A world waited for her to get back on board whether or not she was ready.

'You'll still come and see us?' Joyce's voice wavered. 'There's things of Danny's still to sort out, things I'm sure he'd have wanted you to have.'

'Of course I'll come and see you,' Bella answered, grateful for the taxi hooting outside, wanting to go before she broke down, guilt layering guilt for the emotions coursing through her, the sense of relief that was surely out of place at Danny's funeral. Her eyes were suddenly drawn to a photo on the hall table, a photo she herself had taken on a sandy Torquay beach. Danny, his body salty and wet from the surf, glistening in the sun, a surfboard under his arm, a cheeky grin firmly in place. She could almost hear his voice calling to her to hurry up and take the photo so he could get back out and catch a wave. The guilt disappeared then as she realized that the relief she felt wasn't just for herself, but for Danny.

That finally it was over for him, that finally he was free.

'Take it.' Joyce picked up the photo and handed it to her and Bella accepted with a grateful nod, embracing the woman again, holding her more naturally now and wishing for a futile moment that it could all have somehow been different.

Paying the taxi, clutching her precious photo, Bella made her way through the staff car park, her eyes constantly drawn to the red arrows that showed the way toward Emergency. She was filled with an almost mawkish need to head over there, to say hello and goodbye to the friends she'd made, yet utterly unsure of her reception. Fiddling in her bag for her keys, she located her tired old red car, groaning out loud as she saw the parking ticket under her windscreen, absolutely the last thing she needed on today of all days. But lifting up her windscreen wiper, opening the plastic cover, her scowl faded into a smile, her eyes blurring as she read the simple message: 'Don't be a stranger—come in for a coffee. The guys and gals in Emergency.'

Hands shaking, Bella loaded her bag and photo into the car, retrieved a lipstick and dragged a comb through her hair before shakily walking back through the car park As nervous as she'd been on her first day there, she waited for the sliding doors to open, swallowing hard as she stepped inside, despite the note, utterly unsure of her reception.

'Bella!'

The single word seemed to be coming at her from all directions, smiles coming from every corner, hands waving as she made her way over to the nurses' station.

'Hello, you!' Hannah's smile was the widest of all. She put down her pen and stood up, embracing Bella in a hug she really needed. 'I don't suppose you're free for a night shift tonight?'

'I hope you're joking.' Bella's voice was shaky but her eyes were working overtime, scanning the department, trying to locate the one face she really needed to see, then realizing with a sinking feeling that Heath wasn't around. 'How come you're on days?'

'You're looking at the very new unit manager.' Hannah beamed. 'I don't have to tell you the difference this is going to make to Ken and me. And how's Jayne?'

The crowd of nurses fell silent, loyalty, however misplaced, still there for their former boss.

'She should be OK,' Bella said softly. 'She's got a good solicitor and with a bit of luck...' Bella shrugged. The court's decision wasn't hers to pre-empt, but like everyone else present she prayed it would go well.

'And how are you?' Hannah's eyed raked over the black suit, coming to rest on Bella's red, swollen eyes. 'This can't have been the easiest week in your life.'

'I'll be OK.' Tears were dangerously close now. She suddenly filled with a sense of anticlimax, the world carrying right on just as Bella had predicted it would. Danny gone with barely a blip on the Richter scale, no one, not even Jayne, indispensable in the world of nursing, and Heath painfully silent when she'd needed him most. 'I'd better go.'

'You'll come in and see us?' Hannah checked, but Bella just gave a noncommittal shrug. She wasn't Jim, with a lifetime of history in the department—there was no point kidding herself she was really going to be missed. 'No doubt I'll bring in a prisoner one day, and I'll expect the red carpet treatment.'

'You've got it.' Hannah smiled and even though it was Bella instigating her departure she felt as if she were being prized away, wanted to cling to the walls almost, to hold out to see the one person who could make this wretched day better. 'But before you go, there's someone who I know would love to see you.'

A nervous, tremulous smile broke out on Bella's lips, but her faint hope was soon dashed as Hannah spoke on.

'Lucy O'Keefe. She's still on the obs ward.'

Somehow Bella kept her smile in place, somehow she nodded and made a bit more small talk before heading to the obs ward, a visit with Lucy the last thing she needed today of all days. Her emotions so raw she didn't know if she could get through even a five-minute visit without breaking down.

'Well, if it isn't the sexy young detective come to see me!'

Blinking in surprise at the jovial greeting, Bella's smile was less forced as she walked over to Lucy's bedside. A bright cerise headscarf was firmly knotted on her head, a smear of lipstick on her smiling face, and as she put down the magazine she was reading, Bella noticed the beautifully manicured nails, all carefully painted a vivid coral that clashed beautifully with her headscarf. She looked like some tiny exotic bird, sitting daintily in the hospital bed, and despite her initial reluctance, Bella realized that she was actually glad she'd come to say hello.

Lucy O'Keefe somehow always managed to put a smile on her face.

'Hannah did them,' Lucy said, following Bella's gaze. 'But enough about me, I want to hear about you. You'd never believe the stories I'm hearing.'

Bella could just imagine. The nurses in Emergency weren't exactly known for their tact or discreet remarks. 'You're looking well,' Bella ventured.

'I'm feeling grand actually. Patrick's going great guns, the doctor thinks he should be discharged in a few days and Marnie's giving them a run for their money on the children's ward. We're going to be in Melbourne for a while, though. It doesn't look as if we'll be able to fly home for ages.' Her eyes raked over Bella's dark suit, a sympathetic smile flickering on Lucy's face. 'Where have you been, pet?'

When Bella didn't answer, Lucy took her hand.

'Things really haven't been easy for you, have they?'

'I'm sorry.' A thick out-of-place tear trickled down her cheek, and Bella felt her cheeks redden as she tried to hold it back, not wanting to add to this poor woman's grief for a single second.

'For what?' Lucy chided. 'There's nothing wrong with tears, Bella. I've shed more than my share, I can tell you. But I'll tell you something I've learned, shall I?' She didn't wait for Bella to answer, barely pausing for breath before carrying on. 'Just when you think things can't get any worse, just when you think the world's the cruellest of places, something's sent to remind you just how good it can be. A sunset, a piece of toast when you haven't been able to eat in days, a shrinking tumour…' Her voice stilled for a moment as her news sank in, her smile waiting for Bella when finally she looked up. 'It's shrinking. Heath ordered a CT for my extensive bruising.' She gave a wry laugh. 'I've had worse from netball. Anyway, to cut a long story short, there's a bit of hope, which is a lot more than there's been for a long time. Dr Jenkins has spoken with my oncologist and he's going to take on my treatment while I'm here. And best of all, it's covered. Heath got on to Admin and apparently there are some reciprocal rights that mean I can be treated. I don't really understand and I don't really care, it's all just wonderful news.'

And it was. Bella's smile was completely genuine as she hugged a patient who had somehow, somewhere along the way definitely become a friend.

'Are you off to see your man now?' Lucy asked, grinning as Bella blushed. 'And don't try and talk your way out of it. I've heard all the talk.'

'Which part?' Bella groaned.

'Well,' Lucy started, clearly settling in for an extended gossip. 'Apparently you were seen at the social club, and the next thing Heath's lost his temper in the changing room. Am I right in guessing he didn't know you had another job?'

Bella glumly nodded.

'Sure, we women are allowed to have a few secrets,' Lucy tutted.

'Not at the start of a relationship,' Bella refuted, but Lucy just laughed.

'That's the best time to keep a secret,' Lucy said in a theatrical whisper. 'I'll go to my grave with Patrick thinking he was my one and only.'

'Lucy!' Bella squealed.

'And I'm sure I'm not alone. Men just like to think they've got us all worked out. His ego's bruised, that's all. Now, don't you dare leave without giving me your phone number.'

Happily Bella wrote it down. Funny how on such a gloomy day she'd made what she just knew would be a close friend.

'You take care.' Lucy smiled, tired now and resting back on her pillow. 'And don't fret, he'll soon come around.'

If only Bella could be so sure. She heard his footsteps coming up behind her, and could sense his awkwardness, the slight air of detachment in his voice as he called out to her.

'Leaving without saying goodbye?'

And there he was, blond hair white under the fluorescent lights, his complexion a touch paler than she remembered.

'I just…' Her voice trailed off, words failing her when she needed them most. She felt his eyes taking in her outfit and coming to the same conclusion Lucy had.

'How was the funeral?'

'Awful.' Bella gave a wan smile. 'Although everyone kept insisting at the wake how wonderful it had been, what a magnificent send-off Danny had had, but I'd say ''awful'' just about sums it up.'

'Did you come to pick up the car?'

Bella nodded. 'I got the note on the windscreen and thought I'd come in and say hi to Hannah and the girls. I saw Lucy as well. It's good news, isn't it?'

'Great,' Heath agreed, without adding anything further. His eyes were definitely guarded, the polite small talk over, and she could almost feel his discomfort, wishing she knew how to end it, how to simply tell her legs to walk away.

'I'd better go,' Bella said, and her silent prayer went unanswered as Heath gave an understanding nod.

'Me, too. It's been pretty busy.'

And there was nothing she could do but say goodbye, the writing so large on the wall she'd have to be blind not to read it. Whatever they had started had clearly already ended.

Her lie by omission was just too big for a new relationship to bear.

'Do you want a coffee?' Heart stilling, she looked up at him, but Heath didn't meet her eyes and even though a coffee was the last thing she wanted now, dumbly Bella nodded, following him into his tiny office and staring at the chaos as he closed the door behind them. Papers billowed on his desk, bookcases overflowed with books, coffee mugs littered every piece of available surface.

'I lied to you as well that night.' His back was to her so she couldn't read his expression. 'I'm actually the untidiest guy you're ever likely to meet. It drove Jackie to distraction.'

'But your house is spotless.'

'I have a cleaner—every day,' Heath added, pouring coffee out of the percolator and spooning sugar into it with a hand that was far from steady. 'I guess I was trying to impress you.'

'I'm sorry I couldn't tell you.' Accepting the cup he was holding out to her, Bella wrapped her hands around it. 'I admit I wanted to, but I simply couldn't, the same way you'd never betray a patient's confidence whatever the personal cost.'

'I know,' Heath answered simply, and something flared inside as he finally managed to look at her. 'I knew the second you walked into the police station that you had been right not to tell me. Yes, I think I might somehow have tried to warn Jayne, and even if I'd managed not to, I'd probably have acted differently. I just need to be sure of one thing…' He swallowed hard and Bella didn't make him finish, knowing what was on his mind.

'I knew it wasn't you,' Bella whispered, and now it was her turn to ask the hard questions, her turn to lift accusing eyes to his.

'Why didn't you call, Heath? Why, when you surely knew I needed you to be there for me, did you choose to stay away? I know you must have been hurting, but did you need to punish me?'

'Bella!' Aghast, he captured her chin, forced her eyes back up to look at him. 'You really think I was trying to punish you? I was trying to help you...'

'Help me?' Bella gasped. 'By keeping away from me? This has been the hardest week of my life. I've been trying to mourn Danny and all I could think of was you.'

'Not all,' Heath suggested gently, and Bella nodded, giving in to the tears, allowing herself to lean on him for a moment, to draw comfort from the arms that were wrapped around her.

'I'm going to miss him for ever.'

'I know,' Heath soothed. 'I know you will, and I've been dying to call and see how you're doing. I've driven past your flat more times than I can count, wanting so much to come in, to see how you were doing, to be there for you.'

'Then why didn't you?'

'Jackie.' The single word stilled her. 'I never thought I'd be asking my ex-wife for advice about my love life, but I didn't know who else to talk to. I asked her what she thought I should do.'

'And what did she say?' A tiny smile flickered on the edge of Bella's lips despite her tears, as she heard this confident, self-assured man falter. But Heath couldn't see it, her face firmly nestled in his chest and quite happy to stay there.

'That you probably needed space, that I should hold back for a while, give you time to sort out things in your mind. And it made sense. After all, when Danny was dying you asked me to leave.'

'I did that for Danny,' Bella said softly. 'And when you dropped me off at the station I was too tired and too upset to argue my point about being undercover, but I still wanted you near.'

'You told me to go home,' Heath pointed out, lifting her chin and gazing down at her. 'You said that was what you wanted.'

'I lied,' Bella admitted, only this time happily so.

'We'll take things very slowly.' He was showering her face with kisses as he spoke. 'There's absolutely no need to rush things.' His lips met her frown. 'What have I said wrong now?'

'More advice from Jackie?' Wriggling free, she fixed him with her best version of a firm stare even though her heart was soaring.

'So I guess if we're going to take things slowly, that rules out any deep and meaningful conversations, Heath, and perhaps we should limit seeing each other to once or twice a week, just to be safe.' She registered his horrified face before she threw in her final card. 'And I assume if we're taking things slowly, that means no sex as well?'

Finally, he was lost for words, but Bella had enough for both of them.

'I hate to state the obvious, Heath, but Jackie's probably the last person you should be going to for advice on your love life. You two didn't make it, remember?'

'But we're going to.' It was a statement, not a question. He pulled her back into arms as welcoming and familiar as if she'd been waiting for them for a lifetime and said it again because it was the one thing she really needed to hear.

'We're going to make this work, Bella.'

EPILOGUE

'So much for taking things slowly.'

Staring down at the perfect features of her newborn daughter, who had arrived two weeks early, Bella could scarcely comprehend that they hadn't even been together a full nine months yet, that so very much had happened in such a short time.

The Pill, as Bella had found out, was not really designed for a trainee detective who hit the sink to brush her teeth at any given time of the day, night shifts, extended stake-outs and a love life turned up full blast, not exactly conducive to the rather narrow window of time the Pill required to be effective.

'She was worth the wait,' Heath teased lightly, more than happy to escape the thrum of Emergency downstairs and take the lift to the fourth floor maternity ward to take an ex-

276

tended afternoon coffee-break. Climbing up on the hospital bed beside her, he joined Bella in an indulgent gaze at their precious baby, wrapped in a gorgeous bunny rug covered in swirling bright red and orange patterns with not a hint of pastel in sight. 'Where did this come from?'

'Lucy left it when she went back to Ireland. She left two actually. There was a gorgeous turquoise one in case it was a boy.'

Heath gave a slightly startled look. 'Well, thank heavens it wasn't, then!' Wrapping an arm around her shoulder and pulling her in for a cuddle, he rested back on the pillow beside her. 'You miss her, don't you?'

'I guess,' Bella admitted. Lucy had been a tower of strength when Bella had found out she was pregnant, completely sympathetic to Bella's constant nausea and more than happy to terrify her with stories of Marnie's incredibly colourful birth! 'I mean, I'm happy she's well and home, but I kind of liked having her around.'

'You'll see her again. It's not as if she's on…' He laughed at his own *faux pas*. 'OK, she *is* on the other side of the world. But I'm sure she'll come back to Australia for a holiday.'

'As if her insurance company's ever going to let her leave the country again.'

'I guess,' Heath admitted, kissing the top of her head and then resting back on the pillow again. She could feel the exhaustion emanating from him, knew, even though he didn't complain once, work had been exceptionally busy these past few days, not to mention the thirty-six hours without sleep he'd endured, holding her hand during a labour that definitely couldn't be described as short and sweet!

But despite the tiredness, despite the understandable weary edge, Bella knew there was something else on his mind. Knew that even though he was here, even though he'd said all the right things and was holding her as close as he could, she could feel a shiver of distance between them. Something was going on that she couldn't quite put her finger on, a niggling feeling that he was holding something back.

'Is everything OK, Heath?'

'Everything's great,' Heath answered. 'Why wouldn't it be?'

'You tell me,' Bella answered, eyes narrowing slightly as she looked over at him. 'Come on, Heath, I know there's something on your mind.'

'That'll teach me to marry a detective,' Heath mumbled. 'Look, it's nothing, Bella, nothing for you to worry about at all.'

'Then tell me,' Bella insisted. 'Heath, I've had a baby, for goodness' sake, not a brain transplant. You can talk to me about things other than bunny rugs and teddy bears, you know!'

'OK,' Heath conceded, his voice deliberately light, yet he was completely unable to meet her eyes. 'You know how Jackie came in with the kids last night?'

Bella nodded, unsure where this was leading. Jackie had brought the children in to meet their new stepsister and Bella had managed to survive the event without even a twinge of jealousy.

OK, maybe a twinge, when she'd caught Jackie giving Heath a slightly pensive smile over the new baby's crib, but Bella had put it down to the fact that her milk was due to come in and she was feeling a bit emotional. She felt completely secure in what she and Heath shared, and that confidence gave her the strength to push on further, to ask the man she loved what was really on his mind.

'Jackie rang just before. Lily's teacher called her in after school. Apparently she had been in tears during show and tell. Lily had got up to tell everyone about her new sister and suddenly changed her mind and started to cry.' He gave a small shrug. 'I don't know, maybe she's just tired, maybe it was just all a bit too much to take in.'

'Heath,' Bella said softly. 'Why does Jackie think she's upset?'

His eyes still couldn't meet hers. Instead, he stared at the incredibly long but tiny fingers of his daughter wrapped around his.

'Tell me,' Bella pushed gently.

'OK,' Heath nodded, taking a deep breath before finally voicing what was on his mind. 'She's worried that she's not my little princess any more—that's what I always call her. Apparently, she told Jackie that she was hoping the new baby would be a boy so that Max would be pushed out of the spotlight instead of her!'

'Oh, the poor little thing,' Bella wailed, catching Heath's surprised look. 'You didn't think that would upset me surely? You didn't thing that I was going to be jealous of a little girl!'

'I didn't know what to think,' Heath admitted. 'You've just had a baby, it's an emotional time…'

'She's your daughter, Heath. If she's upset then so are you. I'd expect exactly the same for…'

'Her?' Heath finished. 'We really need to give her a name, you know.'

'I know.' Chewing her bottom lip, Bella stared down at her daughter. 'But there are just so many to choose from. It has to be right.'

'We can't keep calling her *her*.' He watched as Bella fingered the bunny rug beneath her fingers, a smile edging his lips as he read her mind.

'I've always liked the name Lucy!' He felt the tiny inward drag as she held her breath, decided there and then that if ever he fancied a career change maybe he could be a detective as well, but perhaps it was only Bella he could read like a book. 'Of course, it would go to the other Lucy's head, she'd insist we named her after the other Lucy because somehow she'd got us together.'

'She would, too.' Bella smiled.

'How about it?' Heath whispered. 'Lucy Jameson.'

'Lucy Jameson,' Bella confirmed, closing her eyes against the soft peach of her baby's cheek, saying the new name over and over.

'And given that it's only right that she meet her famous namesake, maybe we should think about heading over there for our honeymoon. We never did manage to squeeze one in.'

'How will you get the time off?'

'Well, Sav Ramirez managed to swing three months in Spain when his baby was due and, given I'm a fully fledged consultant now, I'd say that I've got a pretty good case.'

'You mean it?'

'Of course,' Heath said easily, always able to put a smile on her face, always prepared to give more than he even attempted to take. And Bella knew it was her turn to be the grown-up now, her turn to make life just a little bit better, a little bit easier for the man she really loved.

Not because she had to, but because she wanted to.

'Ring Jackie,' she suggested softly. 'Tell her you'll take the kids out for tea tonight. You should take them somewhere nice, where you can spoil them both rotten and make them feel really special.'

'I can't.' Heath shook his head immediately. 'Bella, she's only three days old. I can hardly leave you on your own at visiting time.'

'I won't be on my own,' Bella corrected him. 'I've got half the station coming in on their way to the pub to wet the baby's head and you know how much you hate it when all we talk is shop. Go, Heath,' she said firmly. 'Please.'

Unlike nine months earlier, she wasn't closing the door on him but opening it a little further, letting this wonderful, caring man do what he really needed to, safe in the knowledge that he'd always be coming back to her.

'You're sure?' Heath checked. 'It will mean the world to them.'

'Then do it,' Bella said, her voice calm with certainty, knowing this was the right thing to do. It was easy to share happiness around when your heart was already full to bursting.

'You can give me a ring when you get home, or perhaps see if you can swing it with the midwives to arrange an after-hours visit.'

'Lucy and I will be right here, waiting.'

MEDICAL ROMANCE™

Large Print

Titles for the next six months…

February

HOLDING OUT FOR A HERO	Caroline Anderson
HIS UNEXPECTED CHILD	Josie Metcalfe
A FAMILY WORTH WAITING FOR	Margaret Barker
WHERE THE HEART IS	Kate Hardy

March

THE ITALIAN SURGEON	Meredith Webber
A NURSE'S SEARCH AND RESCUE	Alison Roberts
THE DOCTOR'S SECRET SON	Laura MacDonald
THE FOREVER ASSIGNMENT	Jennifer Taylor

April

BRIDE BY ACCIDENT	Marion Lennox
COMING HOME TO KATOOMBA	Lucy Clark
THE CONSULTANT'S SPECIAL RESCUE	Joanna Neil
THE HEROIC SURGEON	Olivia Gates

MILLS & BOON®

Live the emotion

0106 LP 2P P1 Medical

MEDICAL ROMANCE™

Large Print

May

THE NURSE'S CHRISTMAS WISH   Sarah Morgan
THE CONSULTANT'S CHRISTMAS PROPOSAL
         Kate Hardy
NURSE IN A MILLION   Jennifer Taylor
A CHILD TO CALL HER OWN   Gill Sanderson

June

GIFT OF A FAMILY   Sarah Morgan
CHRISTMAS ON THE CHILDREN'S WARD   Carol Marinelli
THE LIFE SAVER   Lilian Darcy
THE NOBLE DOCTOR   Gill Sanderson

July

HER CELEBRITY SURGEON   Kate Hardy
COMING BACK FOR HIS BRIDE   Abigail Gordon
THE NURSE'S SECRET SON   Amy Andrews
THE SURGEON'S RESCUE MISSION   Dianne Drake

MILLS & BOON®

Live the emotion

0106 LP 2P P2 Medical